Bad Girls of the West
Scandalous Sadie
Ravenous Rose
Tempting Tessa
Nellie's Redemption

I0624888

Want to learn about my new releases before anyone else?
Sign up for my New Book Alert and receive a
complimentary book.

Can the Bad Girl be Tamed?

Nellie Robinson's sharp tongue and scheming ways have done more harm to the debutantes in Fort Worth, Texas, than even the newspaper's scandal-loving social columnist. But when Prince Randolph Schmidt comes to town, she is determined to become his princess. But not everything is as it seems.

Pinkerton agent Daniel McClintock is no Prince Charming, but neither is shyster Randolph Schmidt who cons women into believing he will take them to his kingdom to be his queen. Looks like he's found his next mark—Nellie Robinson. When Schmidt leaves town with her trust fund, Daniel goes after him.

When Nellie becomes a one-woman posse determined to get revenge and her money back, she finds herself in danger as she tangles with a man who wants her heart and one who wants her dead.

NELLIE'S REDEMPTION

BAD GIRLS OF THE WEST BOOK 4

SYLVIA MCDANIEL

*D*aniel McClintock leaned against the wall of the ball room in the exquisite Griffin Hotel, looking for the prince, wondering which woman was his latest victim. As beautiful women went twirling by, their brightly colored gowns swishing to the music, he thought of his sisters back home in Virginia.

Would they be so gullible to fall for a man who promised to make one of them his queen? To take them back to his kingdom in Europe? A mystical place that had not existed for nearly fifty years, but what woman would check? The ones that had been fooled said they believed him.

And the prince walked away with their dowries, their trust funds, or their parents' money, leaving them with empty promises. Except for the last father. The last man paid the Pinkertons to find this supposed prince and that was what Daniel intended to do.

The prince's fake reign was about to come to an end and he would be the person to destroy his identity.

His job was to save other women from this humiliating

experience and this fake prince. Time to expose the thief and the fraud he executed.

The music stopped and an older man stood and tapped a fork against a champagne glass. "May I have your attention?"

The crowd quietened, everyone looking toward the older gentleman.

"As you know, my only daughter Nellie is getting married tomorrow and I just want to congratulate her and Prince Randolph on their wedding."

He was here. The man Daniel was after was in this room. Glancing around, he saw a couple with their arms around each other holding up a champagne glass. The man wore a crown on his dark hair. High cheekbones and a straight nose, the man's emerald eyes seemed to gaze about the room, searching. His smile was a small curve up of his lips, barely noticeable. Tall, he towered over his soon to be jilted bride.

The woman was beautiful with long blonde curls hanging down her back. There was an air about her that was haughty and she held herself like a queen. Only this woman would never experience royalty. Only heartache.

Just glancing at her, his heart sped up. No one since Louella had attracted him and this young woman not only made his heart beat a little faster, but he felt this insistent urge to rescue her. To stop this man from hurting her.

To save her from the humiliation waiting at the church for her.

"Her mother and I will be saddened to see them travel back to Europe, but we can't wait to visit them at his home. Congratulations Nellie and Prince Randolph. Welcome to the family, Prince."

Everyone raised a glass and Daniel smiled. He was about to ruin the prince's nuptials, which would never happen.

As he made his way toward the couple, he saw the prince disappear. The man hurried out of the room as he walked toward him. Before he could reach him, his entourage held open the door and he strolled out and got into a carriage.

Well, damn! In the morning, he would locate the man and arrest him. By tomorrow, he would have even more evidence against him. But tonight, he could still warn the young woman.

As he walked back into the ballroom, he saw her talking to some women. A smile on her beautiful face as she spoke of the wedding tomorrow. When he walked up to them, she turned and gazed at him.

"Excuse me, may I have a word with you?" he asked.

She tilted her head toward him. "Do I know you?"

"No," he said. "My name is Daniel McClintock and I'm a Pinkerton agent," he said.

The woman walked away from the women as the band began to play once again. "Would you like to dance?"

Why he asked her, he didn't know. He was there to do a job and deliver heart-wrenching news, but still he wanted to see what it would feel like to hold her in his arms.

It had been forever since he had waltzed. And maybe he just wanted to protect her, but from the moment he'd seen her, he longed to save her from the heartbreak that awaited her. Tomorrow would not be her wedding day.

Her brows drew together and she frowned. "All right."

Taking her hand, he led her to the dance floor and she slid into his arms. Warmth spread through him and he sighed. As much as he was enjoying holding her, she was going to hate him by the time this dance ended. As much as he felt attracted to her, he also felt the need to protect her from this thief.

"As I said, I'm a Pinkerton agent," he started off. "I've been employed to find a con man who has been crossing the country as a prince of Europe. He convinces young women to marry him and become his queen, promising to take them back to Europe with him. When they agree, he gives them a sad story about needing money for his country for an emergency, guaranteeing that once they get to his home, he will repay them. Only he leaves before the day of the wedding."

Her brown eyes had grown large and she gave a hysterical laugh. "You're mistaken, Mr. McClintock. Prince Randolph is an honorable man who will marry me tomorrow."

Why were women so easily duped? Were they so desperate to marry that they believed any man with a story? The image of Louella came to mind, and he quickly pushed it out of the way. Now was not the time to think of how she had tricked him.

"Has he asked for money?"

The woman stopped in the middle of the dance floor and stared at him. "That, sir, is none of your business."

So he had.

"Where is he staying? If I arrest him now, maybe I can get your money returned."

"No," she said with a stomp of her foot. "Randolph is not the man you're searching for. Who let you in here? You are not welcome at this rehearsal party."

People were turning and gazing at them as she started to throw a total tantrum.

"Papa," she screamed. "Papa, get him out of here."

She turned on Daniel, her fury evident in the way her body tensed. Like a tiger, she was ready to pounce.

"Randolph is going to marry me. We're going to be very happy living in Europe with me as his queen. Why are you trying to ruin everything?"

Her brows were drawn together in a frown as she stepped away from him. With a red face and flashing eyes, she clearly appeared upset. The woman was delusional if she thought this man would marry her. But how could Daniel reach her?

"Let me give you my card. When he doesn't show up, you contact me. But in the meantime, I'm going to do my best to arrest him before your wedding. This man has done this before and he will do it again."

She stepped up into his face. "If you ruin my wedding, I will make certain you are fired from your Pinkerton job, do you understand me?"

Oh, she was vicious. How was she going to feel when Randolph didn't show up? He was trying to save her from the humiliation she would feel on her wedding day, but she refused to accept his information.

"Get him out of here," she screamed. "You are not going to ruin my party. Now go."

Several men approached him. One was an older gentleman who must be her father.

"He's not going to marry her," Daniel said, trying to appeal to the civil man.

"What are you saying?"

"I'm saying he's a fraud who has done this to three other women."

Her father's forehead scowled and he glared at him. "Who are you?"

5

"Daniel McClintock, Pinkerton Agent."

Her father shook his head. "Get him out of here. I knew Allan Pinkerton. He would never hire someone like you."

What did the fool mean by that? Sure, his last name was McClintock, but his family had come from Ireland not long after the Pilgrims arrived.

Two men grabbed him by the arm, and he shook them off.

"I'm leaving. You have my card. Contact me when he doesn't show for the wedding."

With that, he turned and walked out the door. As much as he didn't like it, maybe whatever Nellie Robinson received from Prince Randolph, she deserved. After all, he'd tried to warn her, but she didn't want to hear what he had to say.

CHAPTER 2

*T*hat damn man had made a scene at her party and that infuriated Nellie. It was bad enough that her brother, Seth, had been warning her that something wasn't quite right with Prince Randolph's story, but she didn't care.

No, she didn't love the man, but the idea of being his queen sold her. And to think that her children would be little princes and princesses made her heart fill with happiness.

Rich, the queen of a country with her own family of royalty, these roughnecks from Ft. Worth could all get sucked up by a tornado for all she cared. After dealing with them in grade school, she would finally have her revenge. And she would come out on top.

Never again would they try to harm her. Never again would she feel the humiliation they evoked.

"Are you all right?" Helen Davis, one of her girls, came running and asked.

"I'm fine," she said, pulling her shoulders back, determined that no one would ever make fun of Nellie Robinson again.

No one would ever see the pain their taunting caused her. No one would know of her shame.

Carrie Miller, another friend, grinned. "That Pinkerton agent was handsome. I'd like to learn more about him. See what kind of woman he's looking for."

Nellie glared at her. "He tried to ruin my party and you want to chase after him? Thanks, Carrie. That invitation I gave you to come visit my kingdom is now revoked. Go chase the Pinkerton man. See if he can treat you royally."

The girl sighed. "Well, he was handsome."

Yes, the man's dark hair and brilliant blue eyes that had stared at her with pity were handsome. But the news he delivered was devastating and could not be true.

"What did he want?" Helen asked. "He seemed very serious."

"A prince is going about the country offering to marry women and then backing out. He thinks Randolph might be that man."

The girls' eyes widened, their brows raising.

"What if he is?" Carrie said. "You'd be out the cost of a wedding."

"The embarrassment of being left at the altar," Helen whispered.

A trickle of unease scurried down Nellie's spine. She would be out more than that. Nellie had given him her trust fund without talking to her father about withdrawing the money. But Randolph promised her as soon as they got to Europe, he would repay her, and besides, he would be her husband. All her expenses would come from his money and she planned on doing a lot of shopping when they reached New York.

After all, a queen would need the latest fashions. A new wardrobe to meet other members of royalty. Something fashionable and not what she bought in Texas.

"He's not the prince they're looking for," she insisted. Someone stealing from her would never happen. It just couldn't. Not in Fort Worth where she would be ridiculed once again. "Is that wretched Mrs. Griffin here? I hope she didn't hear or see what happened or else she'll put it in her gossip column."

The woman was a notorious gossip and she liked to fill her column with the latest snippets of scandal she could learn. Sometimes Nellie liked to plant things in her ear and have her write about other women in town.

Carrie laughed. "She was here. You put on quite the show for her. I'm sure we'll be reading about it in tomorrow's paper."

Nellie shook her head. Of all people to still be here tonight, didn't the woman realize she was old. She should be home in bed by now. Somehow she needed to keep this story from being printed in the paper.

"Let me go talk to her. Maybe I can appease her. Help her to see that I was defending my future husband from a liar. Prince Randolph is *not* going to skip our wedding. He's not only after my trust fund."

Helen's eyes widened. "Please tell me you didn't give your money to him."

Why was everyone acting all weird about her sharing her wealth with her future husband? The man was rich beyond means and her little bank account was nothing compared to his.

"Of course, I did. We'll be married tomorrow."

The girl shook her head. "For your sake, I hope you're right."

A trickle of alarm spread through Nellie. Maybe her brother was right. Maybe she should have spoken to her father before she pulled all the money out. What would she do if he'd stolen her money?

All her life, her mother had told her to marry a rich man. And that was what she was doing. And Prince Randolph Schmidt of the Hapsburgs of the Netherlands was a wealthy future king.

"Of course, I'm right. Besides, I've seen his coat of arms. His entourage. He is a prince and I'm about to become his princess."

And eventually his queen.

Carrie stared at her, a frown on her face. "Nellie, you've done some things in your life that I worry about you sometimes. Answer one question for me." Her friend's face was serious, her eyes staring at her. "Are you marrying him because you love him or because you love the idea of being a princess?"

Really that question was no one's business but hers and Randolph's. He had not said he loved her. In fact, he told her he couldn't say that until they were back in his homeland. It was a tradition that brides were not told of their groom's feelings for them until they were in their castle.

And it didn't really matter.

No, she didn't love him. She was fulfilling a promise she made to her mother to marry a rich man. And after tomorrow, she would most definitely be a very wealthy wife. But first, the marriage bed, and that she dreaded more than anything.

What if she couldn't stand his touch? What if she was unable to fulfill her part of the wedding vows?

The memories of that day years ago that changed her life swirled like a black cloud in her mind and she quickly pushed it away, not letting the emotions take hold of her. She'd spent many tearful nights burying all the hurt and shame. She couldn't ever let anyone know what had happened.

"Love will come in time," she told Carrie, the girl who thought love was all that mattered. But she was wrong. "We'll fall in love on the ship going to his country."

Helen's dark brows drew together over her green eyes.

"What's he doing in America anyway? Why couldn't he find a wife in his country? I'm sure the women were just dying to marry him," Helen said.

It was a question Nellie had asked herself and the prince, but he told her he came to see America and then he'd found his bride here in Fort Worth, Texas. It sounded corny even to her, but she didn't care. They would make their marriage work. They had to.

A grin spread across her face. "He didn't come here to find love, but then he saw me and now we're getting married."

And she was considered a catch.

The two women frowned. "You've only known him for a couple of weeks. Are you sure about this?"

Damn Carrie for always creating doubt in her mind. There was no way to back out now. Not after she'd given him her trust fund. She needed that money returned to her or she would be poor.

"Very, now excuse me, I need to speak to Mrs. Griffin. I don't want to read about how that wretched man ruined my party."

Turning on her heel, she strode away, wondering where Randolph had gone. All he said was he had to leave and that he would see her tomorrow. Then he disappeared. Maybe his men were going to take him out for some kind of celebration for the end of his bachelorhood.

A smile crossed her face as she stepped up to Mrs. Griffin.

"Mrs. Griffin, I'm so glad you came tonight. I'm certain you'll be printing a big article on the wedding."

The woman leaned in close to her. "Dear, whatever were you fighting with that man about?"

"Like any good future wife, I was defending my fiancé. The man was spreading malicious lies about him and I put a stop to them."

Damn him for causing a scene.

The woman cocked her head and grew excited. "What kind of lies?"

Nellie could see the woman's mind churning like a dog in heat with the news she could spread in her column.

"Now, Mrs. Griffin, I know you love gossip, but it's not something I want to read about in the paper. After the wedding, before I leave for Europe, we'll have tea, and I'll tell you all about the lies that Pinkerton agent was spreading. I'll give you an exclusive."

The woman's lips curled up in a smile. "A Pinkerton agent. They're the best."

"If that's truly who he is," she said, a trickle of alarm spiraling through her. Why was everyone determined to make her question Prince Randolph tonight?

If the man was indeed a Pinkerton agent...no, her Randolph was a good man. By this time tomorrow, she would be his princess.

"All right, dear. You've always been so good to give me the latest gossip on some of the girls. I'm going to hold you to that tea. Let's get together after the wedding. You can give me all the details on what it's like to be married to a prince."

Nellie smiled and took her hand. "Of course. I'll be honored to let you in on all our secrets."

That hooked the woman and Nellie knew she had saved herself and the prince from being the fodder for the gossip columnist one more time.

Turning, she walked to her friends. In less than twenty-four hours, she would be Princess Nellie Schmidt, future queen of the Netherlands.

Take that all you horrible boys in school who made fun of her when she was younger. Who terrorized her and left her hating people. None of them would ever be royalty.

CHAPTER 3

ellie paced the room above the church, her heels clicking on the wooden floor, her white gown swishing back and forth. Everyone was in place except for the prince.

The wedding was supposed to have started thirty minutes ago.

Prince Randolph had not yet arrived at the church.

Her brother was on his way to the lavish hotel he stayed in to see where he was. But Nellie knew deep down inside, he would not be there.

All the rumors, the lies spread from the Pinkerton agent haunted her and her fist clenched at her side. Was the man right about Prince Randolph? Had he made her into a fool once again?

The room was silent except for the whispers in the corners of the room where her bridesmaids and mother had gathered. Even now, she could hear them talking about how to calm her, but she couldn't be restrained.

"Dear, I think you should sit down. Everything is going to be fine. No man would stand up my beautiful daughter."

But what if he was the fake prince the Pinkerton agent was scarching for? What if he had stolen her trust fund? No, she couldn't tell her family what she'd done. Her father would go berserk. Her mother would burst into tears. They wouldn't understand why she had believed in the man who asked her to marry him.

Her gut clenched and she knew it wasn't from pre-wedding jitters. Oh no, deep in her soul, she knew Prince Randolph had stood her up. Made her the laughingstock of Fort Worth. Humiliated her once again. Why did this seem to happen to her more than other women?

Only this time, she wouldn't cower and hide and let herself be the gossip fodder. No, this time she was going to fight.

Her feet seemed to stop moving and she sank down in the chair.

"He's not coming," she said with anguish. "He's left town and moved on to another woman."

Someone else, to steal their dowry. Someone else to promise to be his queen, only to leave her at the altar.

Her bridesmaids, Helen and Carrie, and even her sister-in-law, Tessa, rushed to her side.

"No, dear, something is holding him up at the hotel," Carrie said.

"Don't give up just yet," Helen said, trying to soothe her.

"I'll shoot him," Tessa said.

That response made her smile. In the months since her brother had married Tessa, she'd grown to like the woman.

Tears welled in her eyes. They had been fierce enemies for

so long and suddenly the woman was ready to defend her honor.

"Thank you," she said.

"Your trust fund," Helen said, her eyes wide.

"Shut up," Nellie hissed. She didn't need her family to learn just yet that he'd stolen everything from her including her pride.

The door opened and they all turned to see her brother.

Seth rushed into the room and they all stared at him. He stopped and gazed at Nellie, his head shaking, his eyes filled with pity.

"He's gone. His entourage is still here, but he's left. That man is a liar and a cheat. He's no prince."

The Pinkerton agent was right.

From somewhere inside, a primal scream ripped from her throat and the room resounded with her cries. They probably heard her anguish down in the auditorium, but she didn't care. Right now, it felt like her soul was being ripped from her body.

No, she didn't love him, but the humiliation of leaving her at the altar was unbearable. At least she had not walked down the aisle to wonder where he was. The pain of his deception shredded her inside.

Once again, a man had deceived her. Once again, she would suffer shame because of a man.

Her mother grabbed her and held her against her chest, rocking her.

"He was not worthy of you. Hold your head up high. Someone better is out there waiting for you."

The room seemed to fill with people who rushed in from

downstairs. Her father's face turned purple with rage. Her brother stood next to him.

"Breathe, Papa, breathe." Her father sank to the floor, her brother's arms around him trying to hold him as the older man grabbed his chest.

"Someone get the doctor," Seth yelled. "He's downstairs in the church."

With disbelief, Nellie watched as her father gasped for air. Her mother's arms dropped from her as she ran to her husband, kneeling beside him on the floor.

"Don't you dare die on me," she said, grabbing him and pulling him into her lap. "The doctor is on the way. Breathe. Relax and breathe."

Pure hate filled the empty spaces in Nellie. The anguish turned to rage as she watched people surround her father. If he died…it would be all her fault. She had brought this pain on him.

The doctor barged into the room.

"Move back," he said, pushing his way through people.

Nellie knew what she had to do. With everyone's attention on her father, she stood from the chair she had collapsed into. She moved in close to gaze at her father. His face was as white as a sheet, and he was gasping for breath.

The doctor had taken out his stethoscope and was listening to his chest. "Today is not the day for you to leave your family. Your daughter needs you to walk her down the aisle."

"No wedding," her father croaked, and her heart cracked again.

They were disappointed in her. How would they feel when they learned that Randolph had taken her trust fund? All their hard-earned money stolen by a con artist who convinced their daughter to give him everything.

No, he would not get away with this. Slowly she moved to the door.

Tessa, her sister-in-law, stepped in front of her.

"Where are you going?"

"You know," Nellie said quietly. "I'm going to find this bastard and kill him."

Tessa shook her head. "You don't know how to shoot a pistol."

"Oh, yes, I do," Nellie said. "You may be the sharpshooter, but I'll manage."

Shaking her head, she sighed. "What do you want me to tell the family?"

"I'm going to find that Pinkerton agent. Randolph needed money, so I gave it to him. I'm going to get it back," Nellie said with determination.

Tessa gasped. "Damn, Nellie. If I wasn't pregnant, I'd ride with you."

"No, my brother would be very upset if something happened to you or that baby. In the past, I've treated you wrong. I'm trying to make amends, but if you care about me, you'll help me. Try to keep them from looking for me for as long as possible."

"What about your father? What if something happens to your papa?"

That was the difficult part. If something happened to him, the family would be so upset with her for leaving, but if she didn't go now, she would never find Randolph. She had to trust that God would take care of him.

"Try to find me if something happens to Papa. But if I

don't go, I'm going to lose Randolph's trail. And I'm going to catch that lying son of a bitch. His days of being a prince are about to end. I'm going to steal his crown."

A smile crossed Tessa's face. "Just make sure you don't get hurt. And you've got about a month before your niece or nephew is born. We want you here to welcome them into the world."

"I don't plan on being gone for more than a couple of hours, I hope," she said. "If I go after him now, I hope to catch up with him before dark."

As much as she had hated Tessa before, the woman had done everything she could to get along with Nellie.

"I'll be here for the birth of that baby," she said.

"Thank you," Tessa said. "Now I'll try to block you from everyone's sight if you want to sneak out the door."

After she snuck out, she lifted the skirt of her wedding gown and ran down the stairs. She slipped past the chapel doors where she could hear the crowd of people being told there would be no wedding today.

All she needed was time to get back to the house, change her clothes, and saddle her horse. Prince Randolph Schmidt would soon be minus his balls courtesy of Nellie Robinson.

Nellie would never be made to look like a fool again. Never. And no fake prince was going to get away with stealing from her.

This time, she would be the one to exact revenge.

CHAPTER 4

*D*aniel McClintock sat in a local cafe eating breakfast. The small restaurant was filled with Saturday morning diners who chatted away, the waitresses scurrying to keep their coffee cups filled. Knowing he would probably be on the road after today, he wanted a good meal before he left town.

Eating on the trail was not enticing. Hard jerky and bacon didn't fill a man's belly.

As he watched the people, his thoughts turned to Nellie Robinson. This morning was her wedding day, and he was waiting to see what happened. His bags were all packed, he'd paid his hotel bill and his horse was saddled.

As soon as he learned of her wedding, he would be leaving. This morning, he had gone to the hotel and the prince was not there. He had checked out earlier. But was he at the church?

Soon, he'd be on the road, hunting the prince once again.

As much as he'd tried to warn her, he feared she would have her heart broken. No one deserved to suffer the pain the prince liked to inflict on his victims. Stealing their money and leaving them at the church, waiting to marry him. That was cruel.

The woman had turned vicious once he warned her about her upcoming marriage. And while it hurt him to destroy her dreams, it was for her own good. At least now she knew the truth.

Sitting in the diner, he flirted with the cute little waitress, ate his eggs, and drank several cups of coffee. If his hunch was right, this could be a very long day. Even longer for Nellie.

How would the woman react to the prince's heartlessness? If she had overreacted to him talking to her, she was bound to go nuts when she realized the man had stood her up at the church. Even now, he could see her going crazy when she learned he had taken her money and left her at the altar.

Suddenly a man burst through the door of the cafe. He stood in the entry way and shouted. "The prince stood Nellie Robinson up in church. She's been jilted," he said with a laugh. "She's still available if any of you want a bitch for a wife."

Several of the patrons sitting in the cafe laughed and the women shook their heads. There didn't appear to be much sympathy to what had happened to her. From what Daniel could gather, Nellie wasn't well liked or respected in town. What had she done that the people disliked her so much?

He signaled the waitress to bring him his check. It was time to get on the prince's trail. As he was paying her, he asked, "Why don't people like Nellie?"

The girl chuckled. "Because she's known for her mean tricks on other girls. She's a snob who thinks she's better than anyone else. That girl will never drown because her nose is stuck so high up in the air."

The woman only confirmed his suspicions.

"What kind of mean tricks has she played?"

"She left one woman out at the creek without her clothes. Drove off and left her naked as the day she was born. Then there is Tessa, the woman her brother married. She yanked her hat off to prove she was a woman and caused her to lose the gun shooting competition. And don't get me started on how she spreads gossip, telling Mrs. Griffin rumors about other girls in town. The girl has a mean streak. That one could marry the devil and he'd reject her."

Though it was hearsay, Daniel didn't doubt for a minute it wasn't true. Louella and Nellie had a lot in common. Though, he'd never understood what made Louella the person she was. How did a nice girl become so mean spirited?

"Thanks for the info," he said, leaving the waitress a nice tip.

"Sugar, you come back," she said, giving him a wink.

With a smile, he turned and headed out the door. He had to find out when Randolph left town and where he was headed. If he was lucky, he'd find someone who would talk, especially if they didn't know he was a Pinkerton agent.

That information he liked to keep to himself.

Climbing onto his big roan, he took the reins and headed to the livery to see if the prince's elaborate carriage was still there. When he arrived, several of the prince's men were packing their gear into the wagon.

"I'm looking for the prince," he asked a young man.

"He's left town," the boy said, stepping away from the other men. It was like he didn't want them to hear what he was saying to Daniel and that was a good indication he would tell him.

"Do you know where he's headed?"

"Nope," the man said.

Daniel gave a sigh. "I'm here from his family and wanted to tell him that his father has taken a turn for the worst. I'm hoping to find him before the man passes away."

The young man stopped and stared at Daniel then he leaned forward. "You know he ain't no prince, right?"

If even his employees knew they were working a con that was an elaborate setup. He wondered how many men worked for the prince.

"Yes," he said. "Fooled me at first though."

"Me too," the man said. Then he leaned forward. "Look, I'm not supposed to say anything."

Daniel backed up, not wanting to pressure the man, knowing that often would get you sent packing. "Understand, but his father hired me to find him. Seems he's the oldest and the ranch will be passed down to him."

Yes, it was a lie, but if it got him what he needed and he caught the bastard, then it was well worth lying.

The boy shook his head. "Damn, wish my old man would leave me a ranch. I wouldn't be out here playing nursemaid to a grown man who wears a crown."

That brought a smile to Daniel's face. He reached inside his pocket and pulled out a folded twenty-dollar bill.

"If you'll tell me where he's gone, I'll get out of your hair. Hopefully I'll follow him and let him know about his father."

He slipped the cash to the boy and the kid grinned as he leaned forward. "He's headed to San Antonio."

"Do you know what time he left?"

"Before sunrise. Said he wanted to get out of town before the wedding. By the way, he never intended on marrying Miss

Nellie. He's done this numerous times and these women believe him."

He had just confirmed for Daniel the man's con.

The kid shook his head in disgust. "Promises to marry them, steals their cash, and leaves town."

Daniel tried not to let his disgust show on his face, but right now, he felt so much anger at how the man treated women that he wanted to smash his fist into the man's face.

"I'm sure his momma won't be proud to hear how he's acted," Daniel said, trying not to make any accusatory remarks. "When will you arrive in San Antonio?"

"Two weeks," he said. "We have to go through Waco and Austin. We'll travel slower than he does. He'll be searching for his next victim while we're traveling."

If Daniel could stop him, there wouldn't be a next victim. If he could stop him, the man would soon be in jail.

With a nod, Daniel watched another man approaching. "Better go, someone is coming. Be careful."

"You too," the young man said. "Hope you find what you're looking for."

A grin spread across Daniel's face as he turned to his horse. Pulling out his pocket watch, he figured the man had about four hours on him, and he needed to make up as much time as possible between here and Waco.

Turning his horse, he headed toward the road.

Time to begin the search for the prince. Time to end his scheming, lying ways. Time to save a woman from being tricked into thinking she would marry this fool.

CHAPTER 5

The first two hours on the road, she had sobbed, sometimes screaming out loud at the sheer audacity of the man. But then she had changed her thoughts into how she was going to torture him once she found the liar.

First, she would take his crown and beat him about his pretty face with the fake piece of jewelry. She didn't know if it was real or fake, but he never allowed anyone to touch it, and if he was as big a dirt bag as she thought, he couldn't afford a real piece of jewelry to wear on his stubborn head.

Then she would have his picture put in all the papers in Texas, warning women about the fake prince, telling them how he said everything they wanted to hear and then he would ask your father for their hand in marriage. She remembered the night her father and the prince had talked.

Everyone had been so excited and now she felt devastated from the humiliation.

Once again, Nellie Robinson was the laughingstock in town. Once again, the boys were laughing gleefully at her and whispering behind her back. Once again, the girls were smiling and saying she got what she deserved.

Exhausted, she pushed on, knowing the Pinkerton man was on the prince's trail. First, she'd gone to his hotel, then she went to the livery, and then she went to the prince's team. There she spoke to a young man who told her she needed to leave. When she threatened to bring the sheriff back, he told her the prince was on the road to San Antonio.

She headed out of town, traveling an unknown road.

All alone.

The sun was beginning to set and soon it would be getting dark. For some reason, she believed she would find Mr. McClintock or even catch up with Randolph before night fell, but so far, she had passed several wagons, but no one she knew.

An uneasiness was building in her stomach. It had been the worst day of her life. And tonight, she feared sleeping alone could make things even worse.

Her six-shooter was strapped to her leg, and though she knew how to use the gun, she hoped and prayed no one would try to start trouble. All she wanted was to catch the lying bastard. To see him go to jail. To make him suffer the way she did because of him.

In the next hour, she would need to make a decision about what to do for the night. If she waited until dark, she would not have a fire. Because the snakes crawled at night, she would not hunt for firewood in the dark.

And yet she had never slept out on the road by herself.

Ladies didn't travel alone. But this, she didn't consider traveling. This was a revenge trip. A plan to get her money back and deal with the man who dishonored her.

A lone man rode on a horse ahead of her. It wasn't the prince, but could that be Mr. McClintock?

Kicking the sides of her horse, she galloped forward, her stomach in knots. What if it was a stranger? What would she do then?

She rode up beside the man and pulled her horse's reins.

The man glanced over at her and smiled.

"It's the jilted bride," he said with a grin.

Rage roared inside her and tears pricked her lids.

"You were right," she said. "He didn't show up this morning."

"I tried to warn you," he said softly.

The rage exploded within her and she let out a blood curdling scream. "What kind of man leads a woman on, steals her trust fund and humiliates her by never coming to the church. The least he could have done was sent a note."

The man grabbed her reins and pulled her horse to a halt. "You're not the first woman he's done this too. He doesn't care about you. You were just one of his victims."

Tears rolled down her cheeks. Nellie hated to cry. She didn't want anyone to see her as a weak person. After the humiliation in school, she had never let another human being see her shed a tear.

He swung his leg over his horse and dropped to the ground. Then he pulled her off her horse and held her in his arms.

"I'm sorry," he said.

No, no, no, he couldn't offer her sympathy, or she would be done. She tensed in his arms and pulled away. Taking deep breaths, she tried to calm the emotions raging through her.

"Why are you here?" he asked.

She whirled to face him. "You're going after him and I'm going with you."

The man jumped like he'd slapped her. "No, you're not. No one goes with me to investigate someone."

Sometimes Nellie refused to take no for an answer, and this was one of those times. "I'll follow you if I have to, but I'm going with you."

"And what would you do with him when you got there?"

"I'm going to take that stupid fake crown and shove it up his ass," she screamed.

Daniel started to laugh. "I kind of like that idea."

"Then I'm going to put his photo in the paper and tell women he's a liar and a thief. He's not to be trusted. But most of all, I'm getting my money back from him."

The man glanced up at the last rays of the sun. "You need to head home. It's already late and you'll not make it back before dark."

"I'm not going home," she said with firmness.

"You're not going to travel with me. Women like you are nothing but trouble."

Why did men always have to be nasty to her? She wasn't trouble, demanding yes, but she knew what she wanted and she would get her way.

"Too bad, I'm going with you," she said. "You owe me. You knew what Randolph was up to and you did nothing."

The man's sapphire eyes flashed, and he took a step toward her. "I warned you about him and you refused to listen. You were too stubborn to hear what I had to say."

With a sigh, she didn't want to admit he was right, but she also needed answers from him.

"Why didn't you arrest him? Why didn't you put him in jail

instead of letting him make a fool of me? He humiliated me in front of everyone," she said all but yelling at him.

"Don't scream at me," he warned.

"Today is your fault. All you had to do was arrest him," she continued yelling.

"If you remember, you had me thrown out of your party. You didn't want to hear my warning."

"You should have arrested him."

In two steps he was by her side, he picked her up in his arms.

"What are you doing?"

"You have screamed at me for the last time. No woman screams at me and I've given you a little leeway. But no more."

"I'm screaming at you, because you didn't help me."

"Oh, and now you think I'm going to help you?" he said.

It was then she saw he was marching her toward the creek.

"No, don't you dare," she said.

Splashing through the creek, in two steps he was in waist deep water where he dropped her.

"You son of a bitch, what are you doing? I can't swim," she cried.

He turned and walked out of the river.

"That waitress was right. You won't drown because your nose is so high in the air," he said with a laugh.

"This is not funny," she cried as the cold wet water soaked through her riding pantaloons. "Not funny at all. I'm going to drown."

With his back to her, he said, "Stand up. You're only in about three feet of water. Unless you stick your stubborn head in the water, you're not going to drown."

Tears welled and spilled from her eyes as she sobbed. It was the end to a perfectly frustrating day.

"Crying is not going to make me say yes. Get on your horse and head back to Fort Worth. You're not going to catch the prince."

Everyone underestimated her and she was tired of being thought of as just petty and mean. Time for her to show people she had a heart. She had a soul that had been ripped from her body.

Standing in the water, she made her way to the shore. Her clothes were plastered against her body as she moved to her horse.

No, she was not going home. As she walked, she gathered firewood. Now she had to make a fire to dry out her clothes.

"What are you doing? I told you to get on your horse and go back to Fort Worth."

She ignored him and continued picking up wood. When her arms were full, she walked away from Daniel and laid her wood down. Then she made a circle of rocks, found some kindling and the flint from her saddlebags. In a matter of moments, she had a nice fire going.

Then she began to remove her wet clothes.

"Stop. You can't undress in front of me."

He was a typical male and soon he would agree to let her travel with him.

Again, she ignored him. Soon she was down to her pantaloons and chemise. She walked over to her saddle, removed her bedroll, and took out some biscuits and bacon she had grabbed before she left.

Taking a blanket, she wrapped it around her and hung her clothes to dry on sticks around the fire.

She had a good blaze going as she sank down on her bedroll. By now, the sun had set and frogs began to croak their lonely sound.

For someone who had never spent the night out alone before, she was doing all right. Except that Daniel was standing to the side watching her.

"You are welcome to join my fire, but if you ever throw me in the river again, I will shoot you, do you understand?"

Daniel walked over to her fire. "I'm sorry. But you were hysterical, you were screaming, and I thought at the time it was the best way to calm you."

She looked up at him, noticing how his dark hair fell onto his forehead and his blue eyes gazed back at her.

"I don't want to be calmed. My anger is my armor and I'm not giving up on finding the prince. With or without your help, he will be mine. Not as in a husband, but rather as in the person I will hunt and capture."

Daniel spread out his bedroll on the other side of the fire. "Remind me never to make you angry."

"I'm not going to be a victim again. And I will do every-thing I can to keep him from doing this to someone else."

Did he not understand her pain?

She watched him staring across the fire at her. "In the morning, you'll return to Fort Worth."

"In the morning, I'll do what I want."

With that, she lay down on her bedroll and pulled the covers over her half-naked body. The man didn't even seem to notice. But maybe that was a good thing, even though he was handsome and those blue eyes of his sparkled with a fire that made her want to explore what caused that heat.

CHAPTER 6

The next morning, Daniel stoked the fire and made coffee before the sun rose. They had stopped along a creek and this morning he awoke to the sound of the water gurgling downstream.

Last night, for the longest time, he had lain in his bedroll thinking she was half naked beneath that blanket. And from what he'd seen, her curves were well rounded, her breasts high and firm, her waist narrow, her hips shapely and legs long and lean.

The image of them wrapped around his waist had him almost moaning. No, she was not the woman for him. But she was a gorgeous woman, who from the moment he met her, he'd been attracted to her beauty. And she had a mouth on her that begged to be kissed.

What was he going to do with her?

A beautiful spitfire that refused to listen. One who did her best to hide her tears. Last night, he had heard her crying and his heart had ached for her. The memory of how Louella had hurt him brought back the painful emotions of how she almost destroyed him.

Though he did his best to warn Nellie about the prince, she seemed completely shocked he had left town the morning of their nuptials. But she was better off not married to a man who lied about who he really was.

If only she had believed him that night. But even then, he'd already taken her trust fund.

Suddenly she sat up, looking bleary eyed and stunned at her surroundings.

"It wasn't a dream," she said. "I'm sleeping on the ground hunting my fiancé."

"More like a nightmare," he told her. "Would you like some coffee?"

"Yes," she said, reaching for the cup he was holding out for her. "Thank you."

The blanket slipped and exposed her white chemise and bare shoulder. At least the material had dried and all he could see was the outline of her firm breast.

"I've been thinking. You're not going to return to Fort Worth, are you?"

What was he doing? The words slipped from his mouth and yet he knew she was just stubborn enough not to give up. That the damned woman would follow him to hell and back to catch her prince.

"Nope," she said with a determination he found admirable. "I'm going to get my trust fund back."

As much as he wished he could help her, that cash had probably already been divided and paid to his workers. She would never see that money again.

"What if I bring you your money back?"

He knew even though he offered her the option, she was

not going to accept.

"No, I'm going with you," she said, shaking her head.

With a sigh, he took a sip of coffee. The sun was crawling over the horizon. What choice did he have? She would be not far behind him, and he would worry about her if she wasn't close by.

"If you promise me that you will follow my lead. Do what I tell you and not give me any sass, then I'll let you travel with me to San Antonio."

In the predawn light, a smile spread across her face. "I make no promises about the sass part. I'll do what you tell me as long as I agree."

The woman was already pushing the boundaries. Would she not listen to him?

"Maybe you should return to Fort Worth. You're obviously not going to do what I say."

She smiled. "No matter what, I'm going to San Antonio. I would like your company, your companionship, even your protection, but I'm my own woman and I do what I want."

Shaking his head, he knew the woman was going to make this trip extremely interesting and probably frustrating. And she reminded him of his ex-fiancée so much, he already felt the urge to strangle her.

Could they make it to San Antonio without killing each other?

"If we get into trouble along the road, you're going to obey me or I'm going to shoot you."

She busted out laughing. "You wouldn't dare."

"If I thought it would protect you, yes, I would."

"Well, then if I don't like something you do, I will shoot you," she said with such a saucy grin that it was all he could do not to reach over and kiss her. Those full pink lips were so inviting, and he just wanted a taste.

How did he handle this woman? Even Louella had not given him this much sass. And if they traveled together, it would be up to him to keep her safe.

"Let's just say the first person who pulls their gun on the other one has to do something the other person will like."

She thought for a moment. "All right. I like hotel rooms with baths. What do you like?"

What could he say? All he could think about was that he would like to strip her down and explore every inch of her womanly curves. The woman had teased him last night to get her way and, damned, if it hadn't worked.

"I'll think of something," he said. "Now we need to get a move on."

She stood and checked her clothing that had dried last night around the fire.

"Did you happen to bring any food with you?" he asked.

"No, I thought I would find him yesterday and be back home this morning."

The woman was naive and yet one thing she had not complained about was sleeping on the hard ground, the bugs, or even the cold last night. Fall was in the air, and in about six weeks, winter would be arriving.

"When we get to Waco, we need to get some supplies," he told her.

"How far is Waco?"

"About a two-day ride."

"Let's hope we find the prince before then. Nothing would please me more than to parade him through the streets of Fort Worth with me wearing that blasted crown."

The thought of him riding his horse through the streets was a rather comical one. One that even Daniel would like to see.

"Come on, we need to get going. We're not going to catch him sitting here enjoying a cup of coffee."

Just then she stood, dropped the blanket, and reached for her clothes.

Dear God, the woman had a body that was beautiful and all he could now think about was how he could get her out of those clothes again. Why had he wasted dropping her in the river?

If he did that again, she'd threatened to shoot him, and he didn't want to test her words. He had seen the gun she wore about her waist. And he didn't doubt for a moment she knew how to use that pistol.

As she pulled on her riding skirt, he couldn't help but stare.

"A gentlemen would turn his head," she said, not looking at him.

With a shake, he tried to look away, but couldn't. Damn, she was a temptation. One he didn't need.

"Who said I was a gentleman," he told her.

Looking up, she glared at him. "You're a Pinkerton agent. I was told they're the best."

"We are, but we're not gentlemen. We're men. Men who like to admire a woman's body. And, darling, what you're hiding under those skirts is damn near perfect."

She was handcrafted and he enjoyed looking at every one of her curves. Even though she was teasing him.

"Well, thank you. Now stop looking and finish packing up. We need to go."

Already the woman was becoming a drill sergeant, but could he blame her? She was beautiful, and she'd just made his morning.

And, damn, he wanted her.

CHAPTER 7

*N*ellie had known what she was doing when she dropped her blanket this morning. Men were attracted to her, and she knew how to get them to do her bidding. And yet it made her dislike them for how they acted.

Daniel was just like all the other men she knew, including the boys in school. A shudder rippled down her spine at the memory of that day. Quickly, she pushed it out of her mind.

Why couldn't she forget what they had done to her? Wasn't it time to move on and yet she still felt the anger and hurt? And yesterday had just brought up all those feelings once again.

Now her engagement to the prince was the same as what happened in school. Now she hated him with the same passion she felt toward those boys. All of them were liars, cheats, and thieves. Because they had stolen her innocence and her belief in humans. Robbed her of her trust.

All day they rode the dusty road to Waco, swaying in her saddle. How she wished a cloud would cover the sun. Though it was fall, the temperature was still warm, and the trees had not even begun to change. But that was Texas for you.

"You ride a horse well," Daniel told her. "I feared you would slow me down, but you're keeping up."

She wouldn't hold him back. In fact, she wished they would speed up. The sooner they caught the prince, the sooner she could go home. Though the thought of facing the people in Fort Worth caused her stomach to churn.

How would she deal with the humiliation this time?

"Don't worry about me. I was taught how to ride and I know how to shoot."

What she hadn't been taught at a young age was how to fight, but she had hired a man to give her lessons and she knew how to defend herself now. No one would ever take advantage of her again. She was prepared.

"Are you always so defensive. I meant it as a compliment."

What did he want? Men were generally only after one thing. And it wasn't her mind.

"Thank you. How far behind him do you think we are?"

If only they could catch him this afternoon, then she could turn her horse around and head back to home.

"Depends on how fast he's traveling. We lost time yesterday when I had to stop and deal with you."

Irritated, she turned and glared at him. Leaves from a low hanging limb swiped across her face.

"Ouch," she cried.

"Better watch where you're going," he told her. "Would hate to see you lying on the ground."

No worries. She was a good rider. "I'm not going to fall off my horse."

For a moment, they rode in silence, the flies buzzing the

horse's tail as it swished back and forth. She pulled her hat lower on her face to keep the sun out of her eyes.

"You're right you had to deal with me. I could have continued riding. After all, I caught up with you. I might have captured him by now. Is there a reward on his head? I'd love to collect the money for catching the prince."

Yes, she was being obstinate, but maybe she had earned the right to feel that way after she'd been deceived.

He shook his head. "Are you going to be this contrary the entire journey, because if you are, I'll leave you in Waco."

How was one supposed to act after the man had made her the laughingstock of Fort Worth? Maybe she needed to let off some steam before they found him. Because once they did, she would go crazy and tell him what he had done to her life.

"I'm sorry if I'm not the giggly, happy young woman you want me to be. Being left at the altar by a man who made a fool of me, who took my trust fund and left me broke, has made me a little irritable."

More than a little. Right now, the urge to scream her frustration was strong within her, but she hoped Randolph was just around the next bend in the road. But there were stretches of the road with nothing but empty fields and there was not a man in sight or even a cloud of dust that would alert them a rider was ahead of them.

A grin spread across his face. "Understandable."

With a sigh, she tried to release the tension that sat on her chest like a boulder. This wasn't the first time someone had taken advantage of her and humiliated her. Since school she had taken on the attitude it was better to treat someone the way you were often treated, than to be vulnerable.

At the time, she swore she would never be defenseless again, but she'd let her guard down.

"Tell me how did the prince approach you? What attracted you to him?"

The memory of the night they met overcame her and she suddenly felt so incredibly stupid for letting down her walls and trusting the miscreant. Why had she trusted him? Why had she let herself be susceptible to his charm? Hadn't she learned her lesson?

"It was at the Cattleman's Ball. He was the guest of honor. Mrs. Griffin invited him."

"The gossip columnist?"

"Yes, but her son owns the Griffin Hotel and the prince was staying there," she said. "And Mrs. Griffin lives there."

"Did he court you?"

She remembered how excited she'd felt that a man of royalty wanted her.

"Oh yes. After we met at the ball, he came to my house and spoke to my father. Then we walked the town together. One night, we had dinner and then it seemed we were together constantly. Eventually, he asked my father for my hand, and I said yes."

"But what about him drew you to him?"

All that time, she'd been infatuated with the fact that he was royalty, and he was courting her. She let her love of being rich and showing everyone in town she was better than them overcome her fear of betrayal. God, she'd been so stupid.

With a sigh, she said, "His money."

"What?" The man stared at her. "Didn't you love him?"

How bad would she sound if she told him the truth? And

yet, she knew from the beginning she would never love the prince. It wasn't the man, but the prestige.

"No, I did not. We never mentioned the word love."

"But you were going to marry him?"

For a moment, they rode quietly and then she replied. "My children would have been princes or princesses. They would have been royalty. I would have eventually been a queen. I would have wealth beyond my dreams."

Daniel gave a little laugh.

"Damn, you were marrying him for the title and he's the one who took you."

"Thanks for pointing that out. You and every resident in Fort Worth knows that Nellie Robinson was made a fool by the fake prince."

Why did she continue to let people hurt her?

"I bought into the fairy tale. I thought he was my Prince Charming." Shaking her head, she grew tense. "Why are we calling him the prince. He's nothing but a criminal. He's not royalty."

And that was why she had let herself grow vulnerable to him. She had bought all the lies he told of his beautiful kingdom. His royal family. The splendor of his palace. Then he treated her like all men.

For once, she would love for a man to accept her and appreciate her for something other than her looks. Maybe someday a man would come along who enjoyed her brain and not just her breasts.

And yet, she often used her beauty to get what she wanted. Just like she had yesterday with Daniel.

"The man is a prince of thieves. He's a ruler of lies and a con artist. You're not the first woman to believe his line of bull," Daniel said.

She had forgotten that he mentioned at the party there were others. She was not the only one to believe his lies.

"How many other women?"

It made her feel better that someone else had fallen for his lavish tales.

"You're the fourth we know of. What he doesn't realize is that the second woman's father hired us to bring him to justice. Whatever it takes, get the man, he said, and we will."

She laughed, joy filling her. "I'm glad. If I wasn't broke, I would have hired you. But he cleaned me out and my father doesn't know. And I can't tell him."

Daniel's eyes shifted from the road to her. His horse neighed and he absently patted him on the neck. "Why not?"

Fear spiraled down her spine and she worried all night that he was not living.

"During the commotion of that morning, my father became ill when we learned that Randolph had stood me up. He grabbed his chest and almost passed out. The doctor rushed upstairs and while they were checking on him, my sister-in-law helped me to sneak out of the room. How do you think I'm going to feel if he dies? I wanted to stay and make certain he was all right, but I had to leave right then, or I knew my family would close in around me and protect me. It was my only chance to get away. To hunt Randolph down."

Last night, she had lain in her bedroll worrying about her papa and praying to God that he would heal him. If he lived, for her father's sake, she could endure being made the town clown. But if the prince's leaving her at the altar was the cause of her papa's death, she would kill that bastard.

Daniel shook his head. "You should have stayed."

Yes, for her father, she should have stayed. But for herself, she had to go. "And let him get away with what he did to me? To my father? Never."

"But what if your father dies?"

Her heart clenched and she felt tears well in her eyes. "Then I'll kill Prince Randolph Schmidt from the Hapsburg Kingdom."

"You know that kingdom ended in the seventeen hundreds and that Randolph, originally known as Fred Matthews, is just a poor man from Missouri who happens to know some history."

So the prince was just an ordinary man with no money. And yet, he'd acted how she thought royalty would. The man would make an excellent actor.

"I'm not surprised. How did you learn who he was?"

"The office in Kansas City sent me his profile. He has done some petty robberies and spent some time in jail. But he's turned into a slick con artist with this new scheme. For a while, he worked for a very wealthy family and learned enough to pass off as royalty. Shame he robbed them before he left."

Rage filled Nellie. "Well, we won't need a trial or a jury or even a hanging tree if I find out my papa died because of him. I'm going to send my brother a telegram when we get to Waco. But I'm hoping we catch Prince Randolph before we arrive in that small town."

"You can't kill him. I can't let you," he said.

"Just try to stop me," she said, looking straight ahead. There was no way this man was getting away with humiliating her and killing her papa. Not a chance in hell.

While it would be painful, she could live through being

made fun of. Years ago, she learned what it meant to be mortified and thought it was painful, she could do so again. But not if her father was dead.

"He better hope my papa is still alive."

CHAPTER 8

*D*aniel rode his palomino mare alongside Nellie's Bay American quarter horse on the road to Waco and wondered about the woman. What made her into the person she was? Why did she act so snappish?

Why was she as bristly as a Texas prickly pear cactus? One touch and you had a finger full of thorns. Thorns that were tiny slivers of pain. Nellie could inflict such trouble.

Yes, he could understand her being upset at being left at the altar, but he was not the guilty party. All he could see was the anger radiating from her and wondered if he had made a big mistake allowing her to go with him.

They had made it out of the flattened prairie and the road was now lined with elm trees and a few wild pecan trees.

The sun was beginning to set and there had been no sign of the prince, otherwise known as Fred. What a common name compared to Prince Randolph. The man was funny to think so highly of himself.

But where had he gone? Had the boy told Daniel a lie when he said the prince was headed to San Antonio?

They had ridden as hard as he dared with Nellie sitting on her horse beside him. The strain on her face was apparent with the dark circles beneath her eyes, pained expressions on her face, and the way she snapped at him.

What would she be like if they were sitting across from one another over dinner? Would she laugh and smile? Would she gaze at him with those brown eyes and bat those dark full lashes at him? Would she turn up those full pink lips and the tiny tongue that liked to peek between them.

A moan almost escaped him at the thought of her.

As the sun was beginning to set, he knew they needed to stop for the night, but what would tonight bring? Would she be sweet, or would she give him hell all night long?

"Let's make camp under that big tree. I'll gather firewood and make a fire, if you'll set up our bedrolls and look to see what we have to eat."

"I'm starving," she said.

"All we have left is hardtack. Tomorrow we can eat in Waco and pick up some supplies," he said, knowing they were running low. He brought rations for one and he was feeding two. The woman had brought nothing with her, but the biscuits and bacon, not intending to spend the night on the trail.

Surprised that she didn't complain about the job he'd given her, he went in search of firewood and took a moment to get away from Nellie for a few moments. He just needed some peace and quiet. Some time alone. The woman could talk till your ears became numb.

But more than anything, he needed some breathing room between them. With a beautiful woman riding alongside him, it was tough to keep his thoughts from wandering where they shouldn't go. This time and space were a chance for him to relax. To remember he had no need for another selfish woman.

He wondered if she would do as he asked. After all, the woman had servants at home. She wasn't used to being part of a team effort and he didn't think she worked well with others, and he wondered why.

Most definitely she was spoiled, but at some point, everyone had to learn to get along with people and he would've thought she'd have learned that by now.

Maybe she was the type of person who never learned to work with others. Maybe there was a reason beside the prince for her anger.

After several minutes, he walked back into camp with his arms loaded with firewood. She stood by the tree, completely still, her face white, her hands trembling.

"What's wrong?"

"Snake," she hissed. "Right by my foot. If I move, it's going to strike."

He glanced down and saw a three-foot rattler coiled up watching him. If he dropped the firewood, the rattlesnake could strike. Her eyes widened as she watched him step backward, his eyes never leaving the coiled rattler.

As much as the woman drove him crazy, he would never wish this on anyone.

"Where are you going?"

"To put the wood down."

"Get over here and kill this thing, before it bites me," she said, her voice rising, her body tensing.

The snake gave a threatening rattle.

"Calm down," he warned her. "He senses your frustration."

She took a deep breath, her eyes never moving from the viper. Her hands were shaking and he feared any moment she was going to move.

Slowly, he lowered his arm full of wood to the ground.

"Don't move," he whispered.

Staying low, he yanked his pistol from his holster and fired, hitting the snake in the head. He fired again and sent the viper flying up.

A scream rent the air as she dissolved into a hysterical, shaking bundle. Standing, in two steps, he rushed to her side and pulled her into his arms. There he held her while her body shook with visible tremors.

"I almost stepped on it," she cried. "One more step and I would have been on top of it."

Tightly, she wrapped her arms around him, and he held onto her. The feel of her breasts against his chest spread a fire through him. She smelled of lilacs even after riding a horse all day.

Wasn't this what he tried to escape? The temptation of Nellie?

Rubbing his hand down her back, he held her while she tried to calm down. Clasping him, he feared she was not going to let him go.

And strangely, he didn't want to release her. He liked the way she felt in his embrace. The sweet smell of woman, the tempting feel of her breasts, the way she needed him.

"I'm not cut out for this. I thought I could do it. I thought I could catch the prince and bring him to justice, but I'm not accustomed to sleeping on the ground. I'm not used to riding a horse all day and I hate snakes."

She needed some encouragement. She needed someone to

tell her she was doing fine and as much as he didn't want her here, sometimes you just needed someone to make you feel better.

"I could have died," she said.

It was true, she could have. If that snake had struck her, he didn't know if he could have saved her out on the trail. But that didn't happen, and he needed to make her laugh about the incident, though it had been very serious.

"No, you're a strong, tough woman and I think if that snake had bitten you, it would have died."

She leaned back and glared at him. "Are you saying I'm poisonous?"

"Honey, not only are you poison, you're downright mean."

Her brown eyes flashed and he couldn't help but smile. This was the reaction he wanted. If she was angry, then she would be fighting. She would remember the reasons why she was here.

Her defiant spirit would return and that's what she needed right now.

"But if you want to give up on catching your prince, I'm sure I could do it alone."

It would be safer if she went home.

Darkened eyes flashed at him, and he knew she wouldn't be leaving. And his words had just stirred the bee in her bonnet and she was ready to sting.

When she stepped out of his arms, he missed the feeling of her embrace. She glanced around the camp area. "I'm not leaving. If another snake comes by, I'll kill it myself."

"Well, shucks," he said. "I thought maybe I could finally run you off."

Staring at him, her eyes narrowed and she licked her lips.

"Just remember if I'm poisonous, I could bite you. You might not live."

He laughed. "That's my Nellie. You're back with that sharp tongue of yours. You're going to be fine."

"Not even a rattlesnake is going to keep me from catching the prince."

Unable to resist her strong spirit, he stepped in close. "And I believe you. The man doesn't have a chance as long as we work together."

A grin spread across her beautiful full lips. "We'll see."

"Not, we'll see. I'm the Pinkerton agent and you're not."

The woman was driving him nuts. Beautiful, tempting, and saucy, and he couldn't resist her any longer. Sooner or later, he would kiss her, but he hadn't planned on it being now.

The snake had shaken him as well and he wanted to taste her. He needed to taste her.

Reaching out, he pulled her tightly against him. He deserved a reward for saving her life. He deserved to taste those full, tempting, lips.

His mouth came crushing down on hers. It wasn't a sweet kiss. No, this was a scorcher that when he tasted her lips, a blaze ignited inside him. No sweet innocent kiss for this little spitfire. No, she needed a man's kiss not a prince's.

One taste was all he wanted. Once chance to see if there was anything between them and now suddenly a bonfire raged.

The feel of her breasts against his chest, the smell of her, and the taste of her lips was so unexpectedly pleasant that his heart slammed into his chest and his dick sprang to life.

Suddenly she pushed him away. "What are you doing?"

Leaning back, he stared at her. "Kissing you. Have you forgotten what it feels like?"

"You're just like all the other men. All you want is..."

Immediately, his body tensed. That stung. That stung bad and he didn't appreciate it. In fact, it made him furious.

"No, I'm not like all the other men. I'm a damn good man and I don't appreciate you comparing me to the idiot you were engaged to marry. I'm a damn good catch, but women like you are too blind to see. You're blinded by money and who is going to give you a good life."

Turning, he walked to the snake, picked up the headless body and strolled away. What she didn't know was that the Lord had provided them a meal tonight. That snake was going to be their dinner.

And if she didn't want her share, he'd be glad to eat it. But right now, he needed time away from the enticing Miss Robinson. He'd been a damn fool for kissing her and he needed to go lick his wounds.

All day long, she'd been a temptation. One he kept trying to resist and finally he broke down and let her know she was affecting him. Only she compared him to men like the prince and Daniel would never be a man like the royal thief.

CHAPTER 9

The next day, the tension between them could be cut with a crosscut saw. They had barely spoken to one another. Part of her knew Daniel was right. She had assumed he was like the prince and other men she'd had to deal with. Because she was beautiful, they assumed she was a loose woman.

And she wasn't. They often tried their best to make her give into their demands. But there were reasons for her refusal. Reasons that kept her an innocent.

Reasons that, to this day, she abhorred a man touching her.

Not even after the incident at school that drove her almost to killing herself had she given up her virginity. But so many men treated her like they believed she would give in to them. The prince had not, but now she understood she was just a pawn in his con act. A victim.

All he wanted was her money and not her body. And she'd gladly let him have her trust. Now she realized why his kisses were bland. Not something she enjoyed and why her body would tremble at his touch. Not from desire, but rather fear.

Maybe that was why she believed him enough to give him her money.

In reality, he didn't push her because he knew he would never marry her.

Did she owe Daniel an apology? Probably. The man had kissed her and, dang, but she liked the way his lips caressed hers. She liked the way he had taken control, and for a moment, she had wanted to lean into him and let him kiss her senseless.

And then she grew frightened. What if he was like all the others?

It was all so confusing. Especially after what happened in school. How did a woman know a man's intentions? How did she know he was decent or someone who would take advantage of her?

But until that kiss last night, Daniel had not tried to press her into anything. And she had enjoyed the kiss, which amazed her.

"There's a lone rider ahead of us," he warned her.

Deep in her thoughts, she paid no attention to the road ahead.

"He's by himself. Wouldn't the prince have his entourage surrounding him?"

"No, he's traveling alone to make better time. They will catch up in San Antonio," Daniel said, kicking his horse. "Stay behind me."

"Like hell," she said, kicking her own horse.

"Woman, I told you in order to ride with me, you had to listen to me," he said to her as they galloped along.

"Shut up and let's catch him," she said, knowing if it was the prince, she was not going to let him get away. For once, a man would pay for hurting her. For once, she would be victorious instead of losing.

For once, she would get her revenge.

They rode hard and fast down the dirt road, the dust kicking up behind them as the man on horseback turned and frowned at them.

It wasn't the prince. Just a man traveling alone.

"Good afternoon," Daniel said, pulling up his horse when they reached the stranger.

"Hello," the man said, staring at them.

"Have you seen a tall man riding a black stallion?" Nellie asked not waiting for Daniel. She had to know if they were close to catching the prince.

"He passed me about an hour ago," the man said. "Seemed to be in a hurry."

Nellie shook her head.

"You looking for him?"

"Yes," Nellie said. "Seems he's not the prince he claimed to be."

The man frowned "A prince in Texas? That sounds odd."

And it had been. That had been the whole allure of the man. She'd been so stupid and foolish for believing his con. Just because a man did not take advantage of her didn't mean he was good husband material.

"Thanks," Daniel said. "Safe travels."

He kicked his horse and Nellie did the same following him. Daniel had barely spoken to the man or even to her.

"Why were you rude to that man?" she asked.

"How was I rude?"

What could she say? She wanted him to talk to her again. "You could have asked him more about the prince."

"I think he told us all he knew," Daniel said. "You were the rude one. I told you to stay behind me."

Didn't he understand she needed to be there when they found the prince? She needed to do something. She didn't even know what she would do, but she couldn't let him get away with this.

Not like the boys in school. This time she was fighting. No more was she willing to play the silent card.

How did she respond to Daniel? She didn't want him to put her on a train back to Fort Worth. She had to continue to travel with him, but she needed to be there when they found their prey.

Maybe for the first time in her life, she should be honest.

"I don't mean to be rude, but I have to be there when we catch the prince."

"Why?"

No, she couldn't be honest with Daniel. She couldn't tell him about her deepest darkest shame and have him laugh at her. There was no way she could explain to him that Fred, or whatever his name was, had made her relive those dark days.

"Because he stood me up at the altar."

"You've already admitted that you didn't love him."

"A wedding is a woman's day to show the world that she's chosen a good husband. That she's given her heart to a man who is going to promise to take care of her and love her till death they do part. He robbed me of that day."

Part of it was true, but some she just made up because she couldn't tell Daniel that this time, this victim was fighting back.

Daniel glanced at her and then turned and stared straight ahead.

"That day seems kind of wasted if you don't love the man."

The man wasn't stupid. No, she hadn't loved the prince, but she loved the idea of the wedding and the marriage to him and the royalty. Maybe she should rethink her ideas of marriage and men.

"Disobey me one more time and you're going to find yourself put on a train back to Fort Worth. Do you understand me?"

With a sigh, she almost growled her frustration. "As long as you promise that I will be there when you take the prince into custody."

"Why?"

Because she wanted to rail at him about what he'd done to her.

"Just give me five minutes alone with him," she said.

"I'm not making any promises that I might not be able to keep," Daniel said.

That was unusual for a man. Didn't they like to promise the stars and then give dirt?

"Take it or leave it. And if you decide it's time to go home, let me know and I'll escort you to the next train."

Now, that, she didn't like. No one was going to put her on the train. She had an outlaw to catch who called himself royalty.

"Why are you so different from the men I've known? You're not going to lie to me and promise me something you can't fulfill?"

He turned and glared at her. "Maybe you've been around the wrong kind of men. I'm not going to lie to you or promise you things I can't come through with. I'm not that kind of man. You need to start looking for better men."

With a frown, she stared at the road, the dust shimmering in the heat. All the men she seemed to be attracted to were men who never kept their promises. Or who humiliated her. None of them seemed to love her for who she was. And maybe that was because she pushed people away.

"If there is such a thing as a good man, they don't seem to like me."

"Could it be your snarky attitude? The way you seem to always talk down to people?"

Did she do that? Yes, she had a snippy attitude, but she only used it on people who deserved her anger. Her ire. People who she could not trust.

"No, it's my *why can't you do things right* attitude."

"No, even last night when I kissed you. You accused me of being like all other men and only wanting to spread your legs. No, Miss Magical Pussy, that is not what I wanted from you. I wanted to taste you, to see if there was an attraction between us, but there's not. I'm not going to put up with a woman who assumes the worst about me because I'm a man. I'm a damn good man who is a good catch, but I'm not willing to accept a woman who doesn't believe and trust me."

Stunned, she sat there. Was that what he intended? But it seemed that all men were only interested in getting in her bloomers. And her bloomers were not up for grabs for any man.

"Trust takes time and believing in someone doesn't happen overnight. We haven't known each other long enough. Even now, I'm not certain I trust you."

"Good, then you can take the train home from Waco."

She was not going home. This fight she needed to finish.

She had to show the prince that she refused to be a victim again.

"From my perspective, men are not to be trusted. Look at what the con man did. What…"

He turned and stared at her. "Who else hurt you?"

That was something she would never talk about with him. It was her deepest, darkest secret and only the ones who were there knew what happened.

"Look, there's the Brazos River. We're almost in Waco."

The water flowed steadily as they crossed the wooden bridge over the massive river.

She refused to look at him, because if she did, then he would know he was right. Someone had hurt her badly. Had turned her against men, even people at the time. And even now, she had a hard time growing close to anyone.

"You can ignore my question all you want, but sooner or later, you're going to tell me who hurt you to make you the person that you are."

No, she would never tell him. Because she would never let him close enough to her to learn the truth. It was her secret that drove her to refuse to be a victim any longer. The prince had awakened the demons and now she couldn't let him go unpunished.

CHAPTER 10

a storm cloud began to build as they rode into Waco, and Daniel could hear the rumblings of thunder. While he had a rain slicker, he knew Nellie did not. They were tired and hot and could use a night in a hotel.

Fall in Texas had almost as many storms as spring. Some of them severe and they did not know what they were in for tonight. Maybe just rain, but it could be high winds or hail or even a tornado. Better to get in, off the road.

A hotel would let them sleep in a bed and even take a bath. And he needed more space between him and Nellie. The woman was driving him crazy, and he wished he could convince her to go home, but something was pushing her. Something that would not let her go back.

Besides, Fred, the make-believe prince might also be bedding down here tonight, and he would love a chance to explore and see if he could find him, without Nellie at his side.

If he could put her in a hotel room, then he'd do some investigating. It would be wonderful if they found the prince here and didn't have to continue the journey to San Antonio.

People were scurrying along the wooden sidewalks trying to get home or wherever they were going before the clouds opened up and dumped rain on them. Lightning streaked across the sky and he knew they didn't have long.

They stopped their horses in front of a hotel in Waco just as the storm began to blow and the evening lit up with lightning.

She glanced at him. "Thank God a hotel. We can sleep on clean sheets and a mattress. We'll be out of this weather."

"Do you have enough money to pay for your room?"

"Yes," she said and he could tell from the way she said it that she probably had very little money.

And, of course, the woman couldn't be truthful. That would be even worse.

Swinging her leg over the saddle, she dropped to the ground. How could such a beautiful woman be such a pain in the ass? And yet, given the chance, he would pull her into his arms and kiss her again. But not until she trusted him, and right now, she didn't have faith in any man.

Not even him.

They walked up the steps to the door of a house on Main Street that had been converted into a hotel. It looked like a nice enough place for the night. As he opened the door for her, she walked through, regal like a queen, her dress wrinkled and splattered with mud.

No wonder she was going to marry a prince. Even a fake one would have suited her style. He couldn't help but think about his sisters and he wondered how his family was fairing. Did his sisters act this way?

Quickly, he pushed them from his thoughts. Thinking of them always made him homesick. He missed all of them.

"Can I help you, sir," said a man behind the counter.

"Yes, we need two rooms," he told the gentleman.

"I only have one available room," he said. "This storm seems to have driven everyone in off the road."

Daniel could feel her tense beside him. Unless the woman wanted to sleep out in the weather, she had best keep her mouth shut. Even a single room was better than sleeping outside.

Grabbing her arm, he squeezed. A grimace filled her face and she frowned at him.

No, he didn't want to stay in the same room with her, but what choice did they have? And she was crazy if she thought he would bed down somewhere else and give her the hotel room.

"Is there another hotel in town," she asked.

"Sorry, ma'am, we're the only available hotel until you reach Austin."

They were out in the wilds of Texas, not in a big fancy town like Fort Worth.

"We'll take it," Daniel said, wondering how they could share a room together. Somehow he would make it work. As long as she didn't drive him to drink. And she was doing that already.

Her arm tensed and he could tell she was not happy. As much as he agreed it was not a good idea, he needed a night in a hotel. They still had a long way to go before they reached San Antonio, if it took that long to find the prince.

It would be good to sleep in a bed. Not worry about bugs

and snakes and even the occasional coyote. A good night's rest was what he needed.

Daniel pulled out some cash and paid for the room. The man handed him a key.

"You can pull your horses to the stable in the back. If you need anything, let us know."

Nellie leaned over. "Could you have some hot water sent up to our room. I'd like to take a bath. Oh, and do you have a laundry service?"

"No, ma'am, there is a place down the street."

Oh great, she was going to get in the tub. What was he supposed to do while she lay naked in hot water? Just the thought made him hard as he thought of all her perfectly rounded curves, her soft wet skin.

He couldn't be in the same room. While she bathed, he would be out combing the streets looking for information about the prince.

If it wasn't storming, that's when he'd search. And she wanted her laundry done. What kind of hotel did she think this was?

A deep rumble of thunder echoed in the hotel.

"I'll run out and get us some dinner while you bathe," he told her as they climbed the stairs, thinking as soon as she was settled, he'd take off and hopefully miss the storm. The horses needed to be put in the stable, rubbed down, and fed.

By the time he returned, she should be finished.

"Who said you were going to sleep in my room?"

Mouth gapping, he stared at her. "*Your* room? I paid for it. I'm willing to share it with you, but you're not kicking me out."

Just then they reached the room's door.

"I have the key," he told her as he opened the entrance.

Inside was a bed, a stand that held a water pitcher, and a screen with a chamber pot. Nothing like getting very personal when you stayed together. When this was over, they would know more about each other than anyone else on earth.

She waltzed in like she owned the place and looked around with disdain. If she didn't want to sleep here, that was fine with him, but he was staying right here. That bed looked inviting after sleeping on the hard ground.

"You know you can't stay in the same room as me. It will ruin my reputation."

Now that was funny. After they had slept on the road the last three nights. She was just now thinking about the damage to her reputation traveling with him could cause. Too bad.

"Honey, your reputation is a cold, greedy bitch, and right now, you're proving your enemies right. No one from Fort Worth is going to know we shared a room. Believe me when I say people in Fort Worth know you would never have sex with me. I'm not worthy enough for you. You want a wealthy prince."

She turned and faced him, her face red, her eyes flashing with annoyance. "What a terrible thing to say."

"Yes, I know, the truth hurts," he said, shaking his head at the audacity of the woman. "We've spent three nights on the trail together. It's a little late to be worrying about your reputation."

He glanced around the room and walked over to the window and raised it. So far, the storm had not broken, but it was growing dark.

"I'm going to take care of the horses and get us dinner. And if that door is locked to where I can't get in, I promise you, I will kick it in and make you pay for it. Do you understand?"

With a sigh, she nodded. "All right. And you'll bring my saddle bags up?"

"Yes," he said.

"Good," she whispered as she turned her back on him.

"Lock the door behind me, but you better let me back in," he warned, not trusting her.

With a last glance out the window, he turned and started to the door.

"Daniel?" she said, "am I really considered a cold, greedy bitch?"

What could he say? He'd promised her that he would always tell her the truth. And when he'd been in Fort Worth, everyone had told him that the prince was marrying the coldest, greediest woman in town.

"I wish I could say no, but almost everyone mentioned how cold and greedy and mean you were. What did you do to those people?"

People didn't turn on someone unless they had a good reason and it seemed people all thought of her in the same way.

For a moment, she hung her head. "Why doesn't anyone ever ask what they did to me? Has anyone ever considered for a moment that I react this way because I was hurt? No, they all assume it's me and not them."

So, something had happened to her. Something that turned her and made her mean as hell. Something he wished she would tell him.

The boom of thunder reminded him that he was running out of time. He needed to go, but all he wanted was to find out what caused her to be this way. What was the mystery behind Nellie's meanness?

Walking over to her, he rubbed his hand down her arm. "Don't ever let people turn you into someone you dislike. It's so easy to become jaded by the ugliness you see and if you let them change you, then they've won."

For a moment, her expression softened. And then it was like she once again returned to the mean Nellie.

"Revenge is sweet and I've become very good at getting even."

Disheartened, he wondered what she was like before. "That's sad. Someday I hope you can find it in your heart to forgive the person who hurt you so badly."

With that, he turned and walked away. The storm was getting closer and if he wanted to do any investigating, then he needed to go now.

"I'll be back soon," he called as he walked out the door.

CHAPTER 11

*A*fter Daniel left, she sat in a chair near the window and gazed out at the people hurrying down the street trying to get home before the storm broke. Was Daniel really going to get them food or was he going to find the prince without her?

Part of her wanted to leave the room and follow him, but then the idea of a bath, of getting clean, of washing her hair and just relaxing was too much of a temptation. If he double crossed her and found the prince without her, she would be so upset.

She would retaliate if he double crossed her. But Daniel was a good man and she felt certain he would not lie to her. He promised he would never lie. But men had broken their promises to her before. Would he be any different?

Tears welled in her eyes as she thought of what the people in town had told him about her. They considered her a heartless, materialistic woman?

Why did no one ask what had made her this way? Because

no one cared. It was so much easier to dislike someone than to ask them what was wrong.

It was easier to think of Nellie as a woman who was bad, rather than their precious sons.

The memory of the boys in school came to mind and she quickly pushed it away. No, she didn't want to think of what had made her such a cold person who pushed people away. As for greedy, years ago she would help anyone, but now, people like the prince had convinced her it was better not to help.

And besides, she could be just as broke as everyone else if she didn't find Fred and get her money back. She wondered if someone had told her papa of her actions, and if even now, he was still alive.

The thought of her poor papa made her cringe. By now, Tessa had told them she had gone after her fake prince and she knew her mother would be worried sick about her. But she was doing all right. Yes, it was hard riding after the man, but she wasn't giving up on getting her money back. Of exposing the thief for who he really was.

Of showing the town people, she was not a cold, greedy bitch. And yet, she had done some horrible things just to salvage her pride and ease her own pain.

Tomorrow, before she left town, she would send her brother a telegram, telling him she was on her way to Austin and she would look for his telegram there. No, she wasn't ready to quit and go home.

The women of Texas needed her help. The prince must be exposed.

She wanted her revenge, but she also wanted to know about her father. Dear God, she prayed he was still alive.

Losing him because of what the prince had done to her would devastate her.

And she feared her hate would cause her to kill the man.

A knock on the door interrupted her thoughts.

"Yes?"

"Your bath water," a man said.

Quickly, she rose and hurried to open the door. She watched as he carried two buckets of hot water into the room. Another man carried a tub.

"Thank you so much," she said and gave them each a quarter tip.

Once they were gone, she removed her dirty clothes. Standing naked in the room, she realized her clean clothes, brush, and even her nightgown, were packed in her saddle bags.

She glanced at the hot water and quickly decided she wasn't going to wait for Daniel to return. She wanted her bath now.

As she dipped her toe into the water, she sighed as she sank down into the soothing heat.

"Oh, I never knew a bath could feel so good," she said out loud to herself.

Sliding down, the water rose to her chin and she sighed. Heaven. Pure heaven. All the aches and pains from two days in the saddle seemed to be soothed by the hot water.

The storm outside suddenly arrived and through the open window the curtains billowed with the breeze.

Daniel would soon be returning, but she was enjoying the peacefulness without him. She needed this time alone to collect her thoughts about the handsome cowboy who didn't give into her demands. And yet he was kind to her as well.

There was a lot about him that she liked, but he could also be frustrating as hell.

Still, it was a shame he wasn't rich. Maybe Carrie had the right idea about wanting to pursue the Pinkerton agent, but she wasn't here and Nellie was.

Suddenly the door burst open and Daniel walked in. For a moment, she cowered behind the screen, thankful he couldn't see her, but angry with herself for forgetting to lock the door. She heard him close the window.

"Are you still in the tub?"

"They just brought it up a few minutes ago."

"Oh," he said.

"I've got our supper."

"All right. Give me just a few more moments."

Oh, how she hated to leave the warm water, but it was time.

He laughed. "You better hurry or I'm going to come join you."

Startled, she gave a nervous giggle. "No, you're not."

"And why wouldn't I?"

"Because you told me you were a decent man. A decent man wouldn't force himself on a woman."

"Who said I was going to force myself on you? I just want to take a bath."

A chuckle came from her. "That I can understand."

She took the soap and wash cloth and bathed. Then she stood and dried herself off with the towel. But she didn't have any clothes to put on.

"Did you bring up our saddle bags?"

"Yes, they're out here on the bed."

It grew very quiet, and she hoped he realized she didn't

have any clean clothes to put on. They were in her saddle bags.

"All right, I'm going to come out in a towel. You can now have the bath."

"You didn't pee in it, did you?"

She gasped. "Of course not. What would the purpose of taking a bath be if I peed in the water?"

"I just wanted to make sure."

With the towel securely wrapped around her, she stepped from behind the screen.

"Eyes down and you can now go behind the screen."

"To hell with that," he said as he began to strip his clothes from his body while staring at her.

"Nice legs," he said.

Shocked, she stood there staring at his naked chest. When he reached his long johns, he scurried behind the screen. She'd almost seen his penis.

"Oh, it's even still warm," he said.

"I told you they had just brought the water."

"Thanks for sharing."

A feeling of comfort cascaded through her. When was the last time someone said thanks to her? Especially for sharing. She couldn't remember, but then again, when had she shared something with other people, besides trouble?

Hurrying to the bed, she went through her saddle bags, searching for her clean pantaloons and her nightgown. But she hadn't brought a robe. How could she eat dinner with him, in just her gown?

Quickly, she took one of his clean shirts from his saddle bags. Maybe she should ask. It would be better than just taking it.

"Would you mind if I wore one of your clean shirts over my nightgown?"

He paused for a moment. "No, go ahead."

"Thanks. I don't have a robe."

"Are you going to wear it to bed?"

She laughed. "No."

"Good," he said.

Just then a boom of thunder made the room shake.

"Did you talk to anyone about the prince?" she asked.

He was silent for a moment.

"Yes, no one has seen him," he finally said.

"Why were you hesitant?"

"Because I hadn't told you I was going to search for him."

Though they had only been traveling together for several days, she knew Daniel would go in search for their man.

"Oh, I assumed you would talk to someone before you came back. You surprised me coming back so soon."

It was true, she'd actually hoped she would have more time alone.

"The storm forced me to get the food and come back."

The rain ran down the glass window he had closed. Thank goodness or they would be cleaning up puddles.

He was being honest with her which made her feel good about him. How many men kept their promise to remain truthful? None that she knew except her brother and her papa.

"If he's out on the road tonight, he's in for a miserable time. It's coming down in buckets," Daniel said and she heard the water splashing.

The thought of him naked made her smile. The man had a

rugged body with a chest that had muscles rippling down. Muscles she would like to run her fingers along.

Surprised, she realized she had never thought of any man that way before. Never.

Slipping his shirt on over her nightgown, the smell of clean man hit her, and she breathed in his scent. How had she never noticed the way a man smelled before now? It reminded her of woods and outdoors and strength.

The shirt smelled like Daniel, who was strong and she admired that about him.

She pulled the shirt around her and buttoned it over her breasts. The tail hung down past her hips. She was basically covered and that made her feel better.

When she married, she would give herself to her husband, but until she had to, she didn't want a man pawing at her or...

A shudder rippled through her. Damn them. The ropes, the darkness, the...Even now the memory shadowed her thoughts of having sex with her husband. Damn them for making her only use men to get what she needed. And now she feared she would not be able to stand her husband's touch.

"All right, I'm coming out. I'm wearing nothing but a towel."

She couldn't become attracted to this man. She just couldn't. He wasn't what she wanted. But what did she expect from a husband? So far, the men she attracted had turned into miscreants. Maybe her taste in men wasn't good. Maybe she deliberately kept away good men like Daniel.

Pushing the thoughts from her mind, she responded. "You come out and I'm going to wash some clothes in the bath water."

"All right," he said.

When he walked out from behind the screen, she turned and they were face to face. A towel covered him from the waist down. The smell of soap and man slammed into her. Heat flooded her face, traveling down her body as she stared at his strong chest. The way his abdomen rippled. The strength that oozed from him. The line of hair that disappeared...quickly, she lifted her eyes to his face.

She swallowed as a fire burned straight to her center. The man was gorgeous. His body was solid and it was all she could do to keep from reaching out and touching his flesh.

How would it feel? Strong and hard?

She licked her dry lips and quickly gathered her dirty clothes. "I'm going to do my wash."

A grin spread across his face. "I'll get dressed and when you're finished, we can have dinner."

Food? The man was talking about food and all she could think about was touching him. What the hell was wrong with her?

"Sure," she said and rushed behind the screen. They could not stay in the same room again. It would be crazy to tempt fate a second time. Even now, she wasn't certain they were going to make it through the night without doing something she abhorred.

CHAPTER 12

*D*aniel watched as Nellie disappeared behind the screen. The woman's sultry brown eyes had widened, and he'd seen the flare of heat in her gaze. They were walking a very tight rope and he feared any moment it would break, and they'd find themselves entwined in each other's arms.

That couldn't happen with this woman. He had suffered with one selfish woman and he wasn't about to experience a second. Yet, he was attracted to her. And no, he would not just sleep with her and walk away.

His mother had taught him to be a good man who did not let his passions rule him and he was doing his best to live by her rules. A decent man thought of the woman first and it was his job to protect her and honor her, even if he didn't like her. But he liked Nellie.

When she came back from washing her clothes, he was dressed and had their food waiting on a tiny table in the room.

"Your dinner is ready," he said. "Probably a little cold, but at least it's not hardtack."

A smile crossed her beautiful face. The woman's cheek bones were perfectly aligned and her pert nose and chocolate eyes were gorgeous. Tonight, her blonde hair was wet and hung down her back.

"What did you get us?"

"The local diner's special for the night. Steak and potatoes with a side of green beans. I know it would be better hot, but hopefully it's at least still warm."

They both sat at the small table. It felt so intimate, like they were lovers on a tryst, instead of working to find a thief. At least out on the road, they had a campfire between them, but sitting in a hotel room eating dinner together in their night clothes seemed like they should be more than just acquaintances.

And God help him, he wanted more with her, but knew it wasn't right.

The hotel room was only for one night. Then they would be back on the road again.

She took a bite. "Oh, so good. I missed having real food."

"Yes," he said, savoring the meat. After hard crackers, anything would taste good.

"Tell me why you became a Pinkerton agent," she said, staring at him in the small space. The storm outside raged on, the rain battering the window.

Part of his reason he refused to share with her. No one needed to know about Louella. She was his private hell and he wanted to keep that secret to himself. No need to share it with a woman who seemed a lot like his ex-fiancée.

"My father," he said. "I'm the only son and I have five sisters."

"Did he kick you out?"

"Oh no, but he tried to control my life and I decided we needed a break from one another. And I enjoy my job. Someday I'll return to Virginia and the family."

What Daniel needed at that time was a chance to show his father he was a man in charge of his own life.

Nellie made him think of his sisters. In some ways, she reminded him of them and how a woman acted, but they were not selfish like she was. At least, they hadn't been when he left and he doubted that his papa would put up with them acting out.

For a moment, she was silent and then she said. "Tomorrow I'm going to the telegram office to send my brother a telegram. Ask him how my father is doing. I'll tell him to send it to the Austin office for when we arrive. I'm worried sick about Papa."

He had spoken his mind about living her father behind and he didn't want to ruin the ease in which they were eating and talking. Besides, there was not much she could do until she learned if he was dead or alive.

They finished their dishes and began to put away everything into the small returnable box.

"That's the best meal I've had since the night before the wedding," she said. A frown appeared on her face. "I owe you an apology."

"What for?"

"When you warned me, I should have known."

There were so many signs and yet she had been blinded by

the prince's tales. So blinded, he couldn't convince her the man was a deceitful liar.

The woman was stubborn and if he'd known her, he would've realized she wouldn't have believed him. At the time, he'd done the best he could.

"You're going after him. What's done is in the past, move forward."

"When we catch him, I'm trying to decide how to make him understand what he's done."

Why did women always believe they could change a man? This fool wouldn't care about her pretty prepared speech. All he'd want was to kill her so she couldn't turn him in.

"Men like him don't care about anyone but themselves. It's all about what he can acquire from a woman. You're wasting your time if you think you can change him."

Why did women always want the last word?

"Change him? I want nothing else to do with him after I receive my trust fund. After that, he's all yours."

She yawned and the storm outside had slowly turned into a soft rain.

"I think it's time for bed," he said, wondering how they were going to do this.

Her eyes widened and she licked her lips nervously. The action made him want to reach out and run his thumb over her plump bottom lip. The urge to kiss her had him standing and putting all the leftover food in an empty container.

She bent to help him, their hands brushing against each other's, and her eyes met his.

"You can't sleep in the bed with me."

"Well, I'm not sleeping on the floor, so you're going to have to share," he told her. He'd paid for the room, and he'd be damned if he was spending the night on the hard floor. "Do you want to take the floor?"

"No," she said.

"Then we'll roll up a blanket and put it between us. We'll share the bed."

"But…my reputation is in shatters. I can't sleep in the same bed as you."

Did she really believe that someone in Fort Worth would care that they spent the night together? Maybe her brother or her father, but the rest of the town would just shake their head and agree they knew she was not a nice woman.

"Who is going to find out? Are you going to tell them? I'm certainly not going to say anything. Don't want the fine citizens of Fort Worth knowing I slept in the same bed as the ice queen."

"I'm not an ice queen."

Maybe? Maybe not, but something bothered her, and he had yet to figure out what troubled the woman. What might be causing her to act so mean.

"Then you better work on changing what people think of you. Right now, you're not well liked in Fort Worth."

With a sigh, she gazed at him. "I've not been nice. But it's a great way to keep people at bay. They certainly avoid you if you turn on them."

The woman was admitting she deliberately pushed people away. But why?

He found a blanket lying at the end of the bed, laid it out, and then rolled it up lengthwise. Then he pulled back the spread and placed it between the two pillows.

"You sleep on your side, and I'll stay on mine."

Her brows drew together in a frown.

"Or take the floor," he said.

She turned her back to him and began to remove his shirt. Quickly, she climbed into bed and pulled the covers up around her neck.

He removed his pants and blew out the lantern. They were alone in the dark in a hotel room with a blanket between.

"We should tell ghost stories," he said, laughing.

A giggle came from her and he was glad the tension between had broken. It was better to sleep beside someone laughing than one ready to throw daggers at you.

"Not if you want me to remain on my side of the bed."

"Let me begin," he teased.

"Do you believe in ghosts," she asked.

"Not really. How about you?"

"No, but I don't like to be scared," she said in the darkness.

"I'll keep that in mind."

"Do you believe in getting revenge when you've been harmed."

He was silent for a moment as he considered what she said. "Depends on the circumstances."

"Maybe someday I'll tell you why I'm the ice queen pushing people away. But not tonight. Tonight, I want to sleep."

Daniel's heart clenched. He was right. There was a reason why she was the way she was. Something had happened to make her so cruel. Something that made her dislike people, especially men.

CHAPTER 13

*T*he next morning, Nellie slowly awoke to the sounds from the street below. At first, she didn't remember where she was and then she felt a hard male chest beneath her hand. Her leg was thrown over his, her body plastered to his side, her head on his shoulder.

Startled, she jerked.

Where was the rolled-up blanket? Did she dare open her eyes or could she very gently untangle herself from his rock-solid body. Oh, did she want to?

Opening her eyes, she stared into his sapphire ones.

Too late. He knew.

"Good morning," he said. "What happened to the blanket?"

"I don't know," she said, realizing that her breasts were smashed against his chest with only her nightgown separating them. The heat of his naked skin warmed her and her breathing felt labored.

Why did it feel so good? What was it about this man that seemed to draw her to him?

"We're not having sex," he told her with a grin. "I don't care how beautiful you are."

She tensed.

"Don't flatter yourself. I must have gotten cold," she said, rising, pulling the sheet with her.

The audacity of the man to think she would throw herself at him. That she would have sex with him in a cheap hotel room. That she would find herself plastered to his hard body, wishing the earth would open up and swallow her whole.

Heat flooded her cheeks. And then she realized, she did not wake up with the revulsion of a man touching her. It must have been because her brain was still asleep, otherwise, his touch would have created that sick feeling in the pit of her stomach. The panic that rose within her that would soon have her screaming.

A chuckle came from him as he sat up in the bed. "Don't get your dander up. I was just teasing you."

She pulled at the sheet to wrap it around her and he pulled back. She turned and glared at him. This sheet would soon rip in two, and frankly, she didn't care. She was going to use it to cover her body until she could reach the screen.

"All right, you can have the sheet," he said, rising from the bed in only his long johns. "I'm going to dress and then bring the horses around. Be prepared to leave in about ten minutes."

"All right," she said, watching him pull on his pants, his back to her.

"Do you want me to turn around, so you can watch."

She made an humph sound. "I was not watching."

With his pants, on he turned to face her. "Of course, you were."

"Not much to see," she taunted.

A grin spread across his face. "Oh, honey, you are wrong about that. But we don't have time to play show and tell. Are you all packed up?"

A blush spread across her cheeks and she decided it would be best to focus on getting out of here.

She grabbed her clothes that had been drying on the screen, folded them, and put them in her saddle bags. "Now I am."

Today's fresh clothes were already laid out.

"I'll meet you downstairs," he said, lifting the saddle bags and walking out the door.

Her cheeks felt flushed as she watched him leave. Why had she rolled over and cuddled with him? What had driven her to his side of the bed when she'd fallen asleep on the edge of hers?

Quickly, she dressed in her clean riding skirt and blouse with a high neck. She pinned a cameo on her blouse and brushed her hair. Pulling it up into a chignon, she placed her hat on her head.

Another day on the trail of the prince.

Glancing about the room, she made certain they had not left anything before she walked out the door.

As she strolled down the stairs, she noticed that this morning the hotel was offering breakfast. Thinking she could pick up something they could eat on the road, she walked into the dining room.

She headed toward the counter when her body went cold and her eyes widened. There was the man they were looking for. Rage filled her as she ran at him.

"You son of a bitch, I'm going to kill you."

His eyes widened when he saw her and a man stood and

stepped between them.

"Now, ma'am, I don't think that's the way a woman should talk to a man."

Swinging her arms, she hit the man holding her.

"Get the hell out of my way. That man is wanted. That man is a thief and he stole from me."

The stranger grabbed her by the arm and held her back.

"Let me go, now," she demanded. "Daniel." She screamed at the top of her lungs. "Daniel. He's getting away."

Randolph picked up his hat, threw some money on the table, and was all but running out the door.

"You fool. He's a wanted man and you're letting him get away. You're interfering where you shouldn't."

"Someone get the sheriff," he said, still holding onto Nellie.

Watching Randolph walk out the door, she turned her fury on the man who had her in his grasp. She kicked him as hard as she could. "Yes, get the sheriff, because I want to press charges against you for getting in my way."

Again, she hit him, her hands full of her night clothes from the room. Suddenly the man let her go and she ran as fast as she could out the diner, pushing people aside.

"Move," she screamed.

When she reached the outside door, she saw Randolph climb on his horse, smile, and give her a salute as he turned his horse and galloped away.

At the door, she screamed. "Daniel, that's him."

Just then the man she was yelling for came around the corner with their horses.

"It's Randolph," she cried and he turned to see the man riding quickly down the street.

She ran down the steps, stuffed her nightgown into her saddle bags and climbed on her horse.

Just then the sheriff came around the corner.

"What the hell is going on?"

"He's getting away?" she cried.

"Who is getting away," he asked grabbing the reins of her horse holding her in place.

Was everyone in this town dense? While they explained who they were pursing, the man was riding as swiftly as possible out of town. Their chance at catching him was quickly disappearing while they told the sheriff why they were pursuing the prince.

Nellie clenched her fists while Daniel explained he was a Pinkerton agent and they were chasing a criminal.

The sheriff glanced at each of them.

"Why is this woman with you?"

"Because he stole my trust fund and stood me up in church. I plan on getting my money back," she said.

The sheriff started to laugh. Why did the man think this was funny?

"My father had a heart attack when he heard the news. Even now he may be dead. I'm so glad we could entertain you, Sheriff. Now may we please go after the prince or do you want us to explain the birds and the bees to you?"

The lawman grinned, stepped aside and released her reins. "Good luck."

They kicked the sides of their horses and hurried down Main Street, hoping to catch him.

"What was he doing?" Daniel asked.

"He was eating breakfast at our hotel," she said. "Probably using my money."

There was no dust cloud in front of them. There was no sign of the man's horse. The road was empty except for the two of them.

After thirty minutes, Daniel pulled his horse to a stop. "He's taken a different road or double backed. We've lost him."

"Damn!" Nellie said, knowing how close they had come to catching him. And now she had not gotten to the telegraph office to send a telegram to her brother.

Tears welled in her eyes and she wanted to put her face in her hands and cry. But she wouldn't. No, she would not let Daniel see her tear up over how close they had been to catching their thief.

"It's all right," he said, trying to soothe her. "We know he's going to San Antonio. The only bad thing is that now he knows we're following him."

Shaking her head, she didn't understand why someone would interfere. Why had the man stopped her from reaching Randolph or Fred, whatever his name was?

"I was within two feet of him and a man stood and grabbed me. He wouldn't let me near him. Randolph walked out while the man held me back," she said, shaking her head. "But I left him with some bruises."

Daniel started laughing. "I just bet you did."

"People need to mind their own business."

"That won't ever happen," Daniel said. "Do you want to continue on to Austin or do you want to return to Waco and send your telegram?"

She turned in the saddle and stared at him in the early morning sun. The man was asking her and that made her feel special. He knew how much sending that telegram meant to her. While she longed to send her message, it would be such a waste of their time to go back to Waco. But it was nice that he asked.

"No, let's keep going. Maybe we'll find him. If not, we'll be that much closer to San Antonio. I'll send my telegram when we get to Austin."

Daniel smiled. "Welcome to the life of a Pinkerton agent. Always on the road, people interfere in your investigation and the bad guys are elusive."

A rush of emotions flowed through her from him including her. They had been so close to catching him. "Is there another road he might have taken?"

"Yes, or he circled back and is now following us," Daniel said. "Let's go a little farther and then we'll hide off the road and watch for a while."

Two hours later, there was no sign of Randolph and a storm was beginning to build in the west again.

"What is it about the rain? Why can't it wait until we're in San Antonio?" she grumped.

"If it rains, we're going to get soaked," he said, pulling out his slicker. He handed it to her. "Here you can wear this."

Gladly she took it from him, but then she felt guilty.

"What about you?"

"I'll be fine," he said.

A rumble of thunder echoed through the land. Flashes of lightning brightened the darkening sky.

"If we stop, we could both get under it," she said.

He glanced over at her. "And sit on the wet ground? No, thank you."

"Well, it was an idea," she said. Part of her felt bad that he would get drenched.

The skies were growing darker and she knew very soon the weather would turn nasty.

"Wait, look up there. That looks like an abandoned shack," he said.

"Hallelujah. Let's go," she said, kicking the sides of her horse.

The raindrops began to fall just as they had settled the horses under the lean-to that would protect them from the weather. She hurried around to the cabin's front as the rain began to come down.

Opening the door, Daniel went in and then he pulled her inside. He found a lantern and pumped it up before he held a match to it. Light brightened the little shack and a scream ripped its way from Nellie's mouth.

A dead rabbit was pinned to the wall with a note written in blood.

Stop following me if you want to live.

CHAPTER 14

*A*t the sight of the rabbit, Nellie screamed. With a yank, she slid into his arms, and he turned her face away from the desecrated animal. It had not been there long which meant Fred had to be watching them or he'd made a lucky guess about them stopping at the cabin because of the weather.

Daniel hoped he was stuck out in the thunderstorm, getting wet. Maybe some of the evil would wash off him. Maybe a good hailstorm would beat some sense into the man.

Thunder boomed and the wind slashed rain against the roof. There were a few places it was leaking, and Daniel just prayed the storm wasn't a tornado, because this shack wouldn't last five seconds against the mighty winds.

"It's all right," he told her. "Now we know for certain the man is in the area. Now we can catch him."

"What a cruel man," she said. "How could I have been fooled so badly by him?" she said, her head buried against Daniel's chest. "Why did I believe him?"

"Maybe you wanted to believe that he was someone for you."

How many women dreamed of leading a Cinderella life? Of a magical prince rescuing them. Had she wanted a man to rescue her? From what?

She sighed and he felt her tense in his arms. He liked the feel of her body snug against his even though he knew he was tempting fate. It was all he could do not to raise her lips to his and kiss her thoroughly, but that would not help the situation.

Already he was way too attracted to her.

But he had a job to do, and she was trying to recover her money.

Suddenly she stepped out of his arms, and he felt an emptiness. He missed the closeness of her body. The feel of her in his arms. The smell of her.

And oh, how he would love to experience the taste of her once again.

Gazing at her, he said, "I'm going to take the poor rabbit down. The prince has provided us a nice meal for the evening."

"What if he poisoned it?"

Taking a step toward the one window, she glanced outside while Daniel removed the carcass from the wall.

The body was still warm and he figured the prince was nearby. The man wouldn't have had the chance to poison the animal and hopefully he hadn't been carrying the dead animal on him.

"No, he didn't have time. I'll skin it and we'll cook him up for supper." Daniel nodded toward the fireplace with old wood stacked to the side. "The man could have had this cabin and I'm sure he's wishing he'd stayed here instead of giving it up to us. Too bad for him."

As he prepared the rabbit for roasting over the fire, Nellie moved about and he was pleased to see she was attempting to help him provide a meal.

"I found a pot and cleaned it out. I thought it would be nice to have some coffee."

"Sounds good," he said. A quick glance around the cabin revealed one large bed.

"Looks like we're sharing a bed again," he told her. "Because I'm not sleeping on the floor with the field mice."

"Mice?" Her eyes grew large, and he could see the fear lingering there as a shiver rippled through her body.

"Any cabin out here like this is bound to have field mice and I'm not one for waking up and finding them gnawing on my toes."

Her face had gone white and he could see her brain over-reacting as she took deep breaths to try to calm herself. "I can do this. I am bigger than they are. We're out of the rain."

A chuckle rumbled from him as he brushed his hands off and stood. When he approached the window, an eerie feeling overcame him and he wondered if the prince was watching them. Daniel would like nothing better than to catch him and return to Fort Worth.

With a fire blazing, it made them a target if the criminal came close enough to peer through the window. Instead of sitting around the fire, Daniel stood back in the shadows and walked over to turn the rabbit every few minutes.

Nellie came over, carrying two cups of coffee.

"Why are you in the shadows?" she asked.

Wisps of blonde hair curled around her face, and he had

the urge to brush them back, but knew that was not advisable. Just the feel of her soft skin beneath his fingers could have serious consequences. It was better not to touch her for his own sanity.

"Didn't want to make myself a target walking around the room. For some reason, I think the prince is close."

Her eyes widened in the darkness and he knew she believed he was right.

"The man's a coward and that would be the coward's way of doing things," she said handing him a cup of coffee.

She worried her bottom lip with her teeth, and it was all he could do to resist kissing her. He needed to banish the thoughts he was having of her.

"Be careful. I'm not a good cook," she warned, gesturing at the coffee cup.

Laughter bubbled up from him. "I hadn't thought of that, but I bet you could heat water if you had to."

"Well, it's hard to burn water," she said taking a sip of her coffee.

He pulled the rabbit from the fire and brought it into the shadows. They had just taken their first bite, when the first shot rang out.

"Damn," Daniel said, pushing her flat to the floor. "I was right."

Suddenly a shot busted through the thin cabin walls, poking a hole where they would have been lying in bed. Daniel watched from the side of the window, the flash of the prince's gun pinpointing his location.

"Stay here and don't move," he whispered. "I'm going to surprise him from the side."

"If you catch him, I get some time with him," she warned.

"You will, but don't move. I fear you could get shot," he said. "Don't eat all the rabbit either."

"I'm not sharing this rabbit with the prince," she said.

A chuckle came from his chest as he slinked out the door.

The man was firing every few minutes at the cabin. Each time, a flash of light gave away his location. Not real smart. As Daniel moved silently through the woods, he found the prince.

He was about a hundred yards from their cabin, a gun in his hand, grinning at how he was taking pock shots at them.

"Drop your weapon and put your hands up," Daniel called.

The prince turned to him and fired, the bullet zipping past Daniel's ear in the darkness. That was too close.

Daniel aimed hoping to wound him, and when he fired, he heard the man scream.

"Son of a bitch," Fred yelled and began to race through the darkness.

He must not have hurt him too badly if he was sprinting through the woods.

Daniel took off in pursuit, worrying about getting lost in the inky blackness of the forest. Finally, he heard the man's horse galloping away.

Damn, he hadn't caught him.

With a sigh, he stopped running to catch his breath. Nellie would be so disappointed. He was disappointed.

Turning, he headed in the direction he remembered the cabin.

When he stepped inside, she was near the fire reheating his piece of rabbit.

"It got cold and I wanted it to be warm for you," she said, handing him the stick. "Since I hadn't heard any shooting, I thought you must have either caught him or killed him? Did you find him?"

It was nice that she had confidence in his abilities, but this time, the man got away.

"Yes, I think I wounded him. But he jumped on his horse and rode off."

Shaking her head, she gazed about the darkened space. "After you left, I sat here worrying that something happened to you. What if you were hurt? How could I find you? Would I continue on alone?"

It was the first time she'd shown concern.

In the darkness, he glanced at her and saw the worry in her eyes. "Yes, I would continue, but I'm glad you're here with me. It would be much harder alone."

It was the first time she acknowledged him helping her and he appreciated her words. He couldn't imagine her alone out here on the road. In some ways, she was a tough woman, but in so many others, she was very vulnerable.

There was a softer side to her he was just beginning to see. And he wondered what had happened that made her so harsh most of the time.

"Thank you," he said. "I don't think he will bother us again tonight. I think he rode off to lick his wounds. But the more we chase him, the more dangerous he will become."

And he was frightened that Nellie was here and in danger. The man would kill her if he caught her, just to shut her up.

"We need to stop him. He shouldn't be able to do this to another woman."

Speechless, he stared at her in the flickering light. The girl cared about other women? Maybe being out here like this, she realized the wide network of criminals. Or maybe she realized her own foolish decisions. Either way, he agreed with her that the prince must be stopped.

"I think it's time we went to bed," he told her. "I finished off my rabbit and we need to get started early in the morning. Tomorrow could be the day we catch him."

She glanced at him. "I laid out our bedrolls on the bed. It was easier if I combined them. There is no divider tonight. Stay on your side and we'll be fine."

Laughter bubbled up. "You're the one who needs to stay on your side. I'm not the one who curled around me. You did."

The wood in the fire popped, sending up a geyser of sparks.

"I got cold," she defended. "Don't be so warm tonight and things will be just fine."

Like that was going to happen, she made him hotter than an August afternoon in Texas.

CHAPTER 15

*N*ellie prepared for bed. It would be impossible for both of them to fit in the bed if she wore her pantaloons and riding skirts and the bulk women wore. So she had the choice of naked or her night clothes. She made the decision to sleep in her nightgown. It would be dark and he couldn't see.

When she was ready, she called out to him. "You can come in now."

He entered and looked at all the bullet holes. "The prince really ruined this cabin. We have enough holes for air to seep in tonight."

She watched as he took his gun belt off and laid it close by. Then he took one of the old rickety chairs and placed it under the door latch. Next, he pulled his shirt from his pants and unbuttoned it, laying it on a table.

Unable to tear her eyes away, she enjoyed the sight of his body being revealed by the clothes he removed. His rippled chest, his muscled arms, the way his buttocks were nice and firm. The man was handsome as sin.

He sank down onto the bed and removed his boots. Last, he unbuttoned his pants and removed them before he turned off the lamp and crawled into the bed beside her.

They didn't touch. He lay on his side and she was on hers next to the wall. They were both tense as they lay there, side by side, in the darkness.

"Have you ever been married?"

"Nope," he said. "When I do marry, I want a wife who will love me regardless of anything that happens to us in life. I was engaged once, but that didn't last."

"Why not?"

"Sometimes a person is not how they seem when you're around other people. I'm just glad I learned who she really was before we married."

For a moment, Nellie was silent. "The prince was not who I thought."

"No, and you were lucky you didn't marry him," Daniel said softly.

But she wanted to be married. At almost twenty, she was ready for a husband and kids. And no one would mistreat her children. She would be one fierce momma bear, protecting them from cruel people. From cruel children. From savage boys.

"Do you want to get married," she asked out of curiosity.

After a moment of silence, he rolled over and leaned up on an elbow to look down at her.

"Yes, I want a family, children, but most of all I want a woman who loves me and puts me first," he said.

What? He didn't want to put the woman first. What was he talking about? She didn't understand.

"Shouldn't you put the woman first?"

She rolled over and faced him. Their faces were inches apart.

"Yes, but in a marriage, each person should put the other first. I would put my wife first and she should put me first. If I can't have a partner who does the same, then I don't want to get married."

In the past, Nellie had only been interested in the amount of money they had in their bank account, the amount of prestige they would give her in society. She'd never considered love and thought marriage was just a union between two families. Two people coming together to live a life of wealth.

"Have you ever been in love?" she asked.

He paused for a moment and stared down at her. She could feel his eyes on her. "Yes, I thought I was in love with Louella, but when I learned how selfish she was, I realized it was just infatuation. So no, I guess I've never been in love. What about you?"

She shook her head. "My brother fell in love with his wife while they were in a wild west show. They are almost sickening to be around."

Not to mention the fact she had considered Tessa one of her enemies, but now she needed to reconsider her sister-in-law. The woman helped her escape from the church while her family was focused on her papa. Their baby would be arriving soon and she wanted to spoil her niece or nephew.

She was tired of fighting people.

"Are they still in love?"

"I think so, they're expecting a baby," she said. It felt intimate to be lying here next to him in bed talking in the darkness. "Are any of your sisters married?"

"Oh no, they are all home in Virginia and none of them are

married. But I hope someday they find someone who makes them happy. I really want nieces and nephews to play with my children."

She hadn't thought about her own children playing with her brother's kids. What a wonderful gift that would be. But first, she had to find a man to marry. And she had to get over her fear of the marriage bed. Her inability to have a man touch her.

"How do you know when you're in love," she asked.

"Well, from what I can tell, you can't stop thinking about the person. You want to spend all your time with them. You want to make them happy and no one else. They become your focus, your life."

She thought about what he'd said. No, she had never wanted to make someone happy. Not even the men she pursued at the balls. There was no one in Fort Worth.

She glanced at Daniel. For the last week, they had traveled together, slept together, and were getting to know one another better than anyone she'd ever met. There were things that made him a nice man and he was handsome as sin.

"What are you looking for in a wife," she asked. "I want to know what a man's expectations are."

"Like I said, someone who would put my needs above their own. Who would have my back, stand beside me and love me regardless of what life threw at us. Someone who would make me a better man."

Her mind swirled with what he'd just told her. When she had considered marriage, all she'd thought about were her wants and needs and they were not on the man, but rather what the man could provide for her. She'd never considered love a necessity before now. She'd never considered what the other person might want in a relationship.

Why hadn't anyone ever spoken to her about this before? This last week being with Daniel had shown her that the two of them had to meld to make this partnership work. She couldn't just depend on him to do everything.

A marriage must work much the same way.

"What about you? What are you looking for in a husband?"

She started laughing. "Before it was all about security and money and prestige. And while that's all good and wonderful, being out here with you has shown me that two people have to work together or there could be total chaos."

"You never considered that before?"

"No," she said, knowing that made her sound so selfish, and she was.

Lying back, she looked up at the ceiling. "Sure, I'd like my husband to be equal financially, so I don't have to worry about my trust fund being stolen again. But I'd like to have a man who made me feel like a good woman. Who stood up to me when I threw a hissy fit, who calmed me and helped me to understand when I didn't get my way. There are very few men who stand up to me. So I think I need a strong man."

A smile spread across Daniel's face. "That's the most honest thing I've heard you say."

Warmth spread through her. It felt good when he said something positive to her. It felt right.

"Thank you," she said, a grin spreading across her face.

A boom of thunder rattled the cabin and she jumped knocking him down on top of her. A groan resounded from him.

They were lying cheek to cheek. He lay on top of her, and

she could feel every inch of his hard muscles, clear down to his…Oh my that was hard and long and fit right in the vee between her legs.

"I said I wasn't going to do this again, but damn, I can't help myself," he groaned as his lips found hers.

Her hands reached up and she folded them about his neck, her mouth relenting to his commanding demands as he pushed inside her lips, his tongue dancing with hers. A moan came from her throat. It was a sound she had never uttered during a kiss and it surprised her.

She could feel his hard penis between her legs and his hand reached down and touched her breast.

The memory like a coiled rattlesnake slammed into her. Her hands were pulled up and behind her as the boys took turns feeling her breasts. Screaming…

Her body froze and Daniel suddenly broke the kiss.

"What's wrong?"

A tear slipped down her cheek. She wouldn't cry in front of him. No, she couldn't. How could she endure a marriage bed if she couldn't or wouldn't let him kiss her?

"We can't," she said. "We've got to stop."

For a moment, he was silent.

"No," he said. "You were enjoying my kiss. We were both aroused and then when I touched your breast, you jerked."

They had taken turns mauling her breasts. They had twisted her nipples and even placed their fingers on her privates.

She couldn't talk about what happened to her. She'd been lucky, but until now, she'd never realized how much it still bothered her. How much it affected her. How angry she became when she realized how they had ruined her. Would she ever be able to endure a man's touch again?

Sitting up, she pushed him away and resorted to how she normally acted when the memory overcame her.

"We're not married. We are not going to have sex," she said in the hateful tone she resorted to pushing people away. Somehow she had to make certain he hated her and would never try that again. Somehow she had to make Daniel realize she was just a bitch at heart.

At first, he stared at her and then he lay back.

"Something happened to you that you're not telling me. And that's your decision. But until you talk about what happened, you're never going to get over this. You'll never have a happy marriage or a life fulfilled. When you're ready, I'm here to listen. No judgement."

How did the man know? And how could she ever talk about what happened to her that day. The memory even now pained her.

"Shut up and go to sleep, Daniel," she said, lying back and rolling away from him. "I'm not going to tell you or anyone."

CHAPTER 16

It was their last night on the road before they reached Austin. Once again, they were sleeping outside with a campfire between them. But Nellie was having trouble sleeping. Since last night, her mind kept returning to the incident after school.

All these years, she thought she'd gotten over it and prided herself in how she had changed and become stronger. Never again would anyone take advantage of her and yet the prince had stolen her money.

People hated her and she couldn't trust anyone. But more than anything, she had a hard time enduring a man's touch. All but Daniel's. He had touched her and she didn't seem to mind until she did. What was it about him that was different? Why didn't she cringe with revulsion?

And now, Daniel was telling her she was not reacting the way a woman should respond to a man's caresses. But how could she tell him what happened? Even her own family didn't know what the boys in her class had done to her.

The memory of the feel of their hands on her sent shivers

radiating through her. She should have killed all of them. More than once in her life, she had wanted to bring a rain of fire on them, but instead she got back in smaller ways.

She was fortunate they hadn't raped her and yet the thought of having sex with a man touching her body in intimate places sent her into a near panic. Daniel's kisses thrilled her in ways she'd never expected. She liked the touch of his hand on her body, and most men she recoiled from. Yet, when he touched her breast, she tensed, the memory of that day filling her mind with a flood of pure fear.

The bastards wanted to take her virginity.

Even now, her chest tightened and her breathing became rapid and she felt the urge to run, but it was all in her mind. Would she ever get over that day? Would she ever be able to look any of them in the eye again without wanting to destroy them?

The faces of the boys came to mind, and she realized that every one of them she had done some kind of harm. Not bodily, but they lost girlfriends, loans were denied, or their names were mentioned for crimes. She had gone out of her way to get her retaliation and it still did not ease the burden she carried.

It did not take away the hurt and she could never get enough revenge.

How could she ever get rid of this pain? Would she ever be a whole woman again?

She glanced at the man sleeping in his bedroll. He was the first man she developed feelings for and that frightened her. Part of her wanted to act like she always did and push him away. And she wondered if her acidic comments would send him away.

Could she act bad enough that he would turn from her?

But did she want him to?

He was the only man to realize that something bothered her. Something caused her to act the way she did. Even her own family didn't recognize something was wrong. And that angered her for years. Did they not see she had been hurting for weeks afterward? Now it carried on for years and still they didn't notice her pain.

The sound of a rock scooting along the ground and leaves crunching had her sitting up and looking about in the darkness. The fire had died down to almost nothing. Was an animal out in the dark or a person or was she just being a frightened nilly?

No longer did she feel that nothing could happen to her. But now she was prepared. Never again would she let herself be vulnerable. Never again would a man or boy take advantage of her. Not even a prince.

The crunching noise sounded again and this time it was closer.

"Daniel," she whispered, not really believing it was the prince, but possibly a coyote or some other large animal or even a perfect stranger.

The prince was probably already in Austin sleeping in a hotel room warm and comfortable.

The man slept on. They had pushed hard today trying to locate the con man, but so far nothing.

"Daniel," she again said, louder this time.

Finally, she reached for her gun and slowly stood, gazing about hoping not to see anything in the dark, but unable to continue lying there without checking.

Tonight, she slept in her clothes. She slipped her boots on that were sitting by the fire.

Stepping into the darkness, she moved slowly through the woods listening for the slightest noise. There was nothing. Maybe she was nervous and just overreacted, but she felt certain she had heard footsteps.

Standing still, she listened to the night sounds and all she heard were crickets and frogs and even a few mosquitos buzzing about her head. Nothing that would cause them harm.

If she didn't get some sleep, she would be dead tired tomorrow and whirled around to return to camp and came face to face with a pistol pointed at her head.

"Hello, Nellie," Prince Randolph said as he grabbed her arm and pulled her farther away from the camp.

Realizing the danger, she raised her gun and he ripped the weapon from her hand and shoved it in his pocket. "No need for you to have a weapon."

Fear scurried down her spine. She had no weapon. She was defenseless and Daniel was sound asleep. What should she do?

"Let go of me," she demanded, but he didn't respond, but hurried them farther and farther away. She opened her mouth and he pulled the trigger back.

"If you scream, you're a dead woman," he said.

Well, she wasn't ready to die just yet. And she feared he would have no problem killing her.

Finally, he pulled her into a clearing where his horse was tied up.

With a shove, he released her, though the gun was still pointed at her chest.

"Why are you following me?"

"You know why. You took my trust fund. All the money I had in the world. The money I wanted to share with my husband."

A grin spread across his face. "It was very helpful."

"I want it back," she said. "Give it back to me and I'll let you go. But if you don't, I'll follow you all the way to hell and back."

A chuckle came from him. "Too late. I've already spent it. A prince has a certain reputation to uphold and I have expenses. As for following me to hell, you're not going with me."

She felt defeated, but she was not going to give up just yet.

"No," she cried. "I want my money back. Haven't you humiliated me enough? You took my money, you left me at the church on our wedding day. You made a fool out of me."

In the darkness, she could see the man grinning.

"Oh honey, shut up. You didn't really love me. You only wanted the chance to be queen. There was no way in hell I would marry a bitch like you. Even if I had a kingdom."

His words were painful. No one wanted Nellie. Not her friends, her family, or even this criminal.

"No, I didn't love you. But I believed you were a prince and instead you're just a common criminal. But don't worry, your time is almost up. Daniel will soon awaken and then you'll soon be behind bars."

"Never," he responded. "I'm not going to jail. I'll kill you and that Pinkerton agent before I allow you to put me behind bars."

No, he was trying to frighten her and she refused to back down.

"Just give me my trust fund," she demanded. "Give me the money back and you can leave."

"No," he said. "It's now mine and there's nothing you can do about it."

Oh, yes there was, and as soon as she could reach her gun, he would no longer need money.

The man gave her an evil grin and she worried how she could escape.

"You're a lousy kisser," he said. "And a cold-hearted bitch."

"Well, thank you, Prince Liar. You're certainly no catch. And now that we've traded insults, let me go."

A frown appeared between his eyes as the moon slipped from behind the clouds shining down brightly on them in the meadow. She began to search for a way to escape.

"Why is a Pinkerton agent following me?" he asked, ignoring her request to leave.

"You'll have to ask him," she said. "This cold-hearted bitch doesn't know."

Suddenly pain radiated from her jaw. The man had slapped her.

"Oh, that proves you're a big man."

Anger surged from her and it was all she could do to keep from charging him.

"I'll ask you again," he told her with a smile. "Why is the Pinkerton agent here?"

He stepped closer and was about to hit her again. What she knew wasn't much.

"Because you're as dumb as they come. All he's told me is that they were hired to find you. Even if I walked away today, they would continue searching for you."

"Son of a bitch," he said.

"Turn yourself in and they'll go easier on you. Give me my money back and I'll say a good word for you."

No, she wouldn't, but he didn't need to know.

"Like that would help me. No one in town likes you," he said. "Your word with the townspeople is not worth much."

Sadly, she felt he was right. No one cared about her word. No one cared that she'd been duped by this man.

Why was Daniel the only one who could see her pain? Why did he understand that she was reacting to something that pained her? Why was he the only one who saw the goodness in her?

No one else cared.

"Then hang for all I care," she said, feeling the anxiety starting to build inside her.

His head swung back to her and he stared at her like she had gone crazy. "I've done nothing wrong. You can't prove it. You gave me your money because I was going to be your husband."

"And now I want it all back," she said. "You'll never be my husband."

Thank goodness for that. After this was over, she hoped never to see this man again.

"If you and your Pinkerton agent lover don't stop following me, I'm going to kill you."

She flinched. "Kill us? Lover?"

"I saw you in the cabin. You slept in the same bed."

Laughter bubbled up and came out. "You tried to kill us that night. I see that big bandage on your arm. Daniel shot you and that's the only reason you left us alone. We're not lovers."

Though as much as she feared having sex with a man, the

thought of being with Daniel was pleasant. Almost like she wanted to have sex with him. But if she couldn't endure his touch, how could she ever be with any man?

"Nellie," she heard Daniel call.

Thank goodness. She'd never heard such a sweet sound as his voice calling for her. That meant he was searching to find her.

"He's coming," Fred hissed. "I should shoot the both of you. And if you don't stop following me, I will. The prince will tell his men to execute you. Do you understand?"

Nellie couldn't help but laugh. The man was totally insane. Why had she not realized this before?

"You're not a prince," she hissed. "You're a thief."

"The hell I'm not," he said.

Just then she saw him lift his pistol and suddenly an explosion of pain radiated from her head as she slowly fell to the ground.

Daniel…

a noise caused Daniel to open his eyes and stare in the darkness. Something wasn't right. He glanced at the other side of the fire and Nellie's bedroll was empty. Had she stepped into the bushes to relieve herself? Where was she?

In the distance, he heard raised voices. What the hell was going on? Jumping up, he pulled on his pants, his boots and grabbed his gun.

As silently as possible, he ran to her, knowing instinctively she was in trouble.

Then he saw them from a distance. It was Fred and Nellie, and the man was holding a gun on her. They were arguing. Somehow he had to get her out of there without the prince pulling that trigger.

Somehow he had to save her, though he would probably lose the thief.

"Nellie," he yelled, hoping it would scare the man to leave. Until Nellie was safe, he would not try to apprehend the prince. Too much danger of her getting shot.

Frozen, he watched as the man raised his pistol and hit her

on the head. She slumped to the ground. Daniel ran as fast as he could, his gun in his hand, ready to kill the monster. You didn't hit a woman. You didn't hit Nellie.

His heart clenched with pain and he suddenly realized he was beginning to care for her. Somewhere along the trail this past week, he had developed feelings for this woman and that scared the hell out of him.

Somehow this frustrating woman had gotten under his skin. And now she needed his help. His protection from the bastard.

When he reached her side, the man was on his horse galloping through the forest into the night.

Rolling Nellie over, he pulled her onto his lap. She was out, her body limp.

Terrified he tried to wake her.

"Nellie," he cried, his throat clogging with unshed tears. She was a mess emotionally and now she lay here hurt while he desperately tried to awaken her.

Unable to resist, he kissed her forehead.

"Come back to me. Wake up, Nellie. You can't let that bastard win," he said, holding and rocking her in his lap.

She moaned and he brushed her hair back from her face. The blonde was the most beautiful woman he had ever met and yet she had more demons than anyone he knew. And he didn't understand what troubled her, but it must have to do with men. Someone did something to her and now she kept people at bay.

It had taken him awhile, but slowly he was starting to understand why Nellie had the reputation she did. And yet every day he spent with her on the trail, he liked her more and more. Hidden beneath that tough, sarcastic, mean exterior was a soft-hearted woman. A woman who suffered and couldn't talk about her pain.

Daniel knew he was not what she wanted and he needed to put these thoughts out of his mind. She wanted a man who was a real prince. Not a Pinkerton agent. She wanted a rich man.

They needed to get back to their camp. Maybe if he put some cold water on her face, she'd awaken.

Standing, he lifted her and carried her back, determined to protect her from anyone else harming her. If his thoughts were true, she needed a man to defend her. To keep the demons away. To help her see she was a kind, decent woman. That there were good men in the world who would want her.

When he laid her on her bedroll, she moaned. "Daniel."

Relief flooded him and he hurried over with a canteen. "Nellie, darling, take a sip of water. Wake up, honey, you're scaring me."

A slight smile crossed her face and she reached out and gripped his hand. "You sleep like the dead."

A chuckle rumbled up from his chest. "You're right."

"My eyes are so heavy," she said, groaning. "I just want to go back to sleep."

"No, you can't," he said, fear overcoming him. "You've got to wake up and talk to me."

She reached up to where there was a large knot on her head. "My head hurts."

"You took quite the smack," he said.

"Let me sleep," she said, rolling over to snuggle back into the covers.

When some patients with head injuries went back to sleep,

they never woke, and he wanted her awake. He wanted her alive. He needed her.

"Come on, darling, you know we're going to leave here real soon. I'll fix you a nice breakfast and you can tell me all about what you and the prince were arguing about."

"He's a bastard," she said, still trying to snuggle into her bedroll.

Her eyelids opened and then slid closed. Again, he could see her fighting to keep them open. Finally, she looked like she was drunk, her eyes were dilated to the size of a nickel and they kept closing.

Her eyes opened wide and she gazed at him. "He said he was going to kill us if we continued to follow him."

"What did you say?" he said, hoping if they could keep talking she would stay awake.

"I just laughed. You've already shot him once; you can do it again. Or I would love to put a bullet in him."

So his bullet had found the man. Good. Shame it didn't seem to have slowed him down.

"What else did you and Prince Charming talk about?"

For a moment, she seemed to doze off and then she came around and said, "He says he spent all my money and that even if I said a good word for him, no one in town likes me. I told him I hoped he hanged. Overall, I thought we had a good talk."

Daniel stared at her and laughed. She must be delirious if she thought they had a "good talk."

Dawn was beginning to peek over the eastern edge of the sky.

"I'm going to fix you some coffee and some bacon. I'm hoping it will wake you up enough we can ride onto Austin.

Unless you're ready to go home, I'm going to continue to pursue the fraud."

A giggle escaped from Nellie and he couldn't ever remember hearing her giggle before now. "He believes he's a real prince."

"What?" Daniel replied unable to believe his ears.

"A bona fide royal member. Next time, I'll remind him he's just Fred from Missouri," she said with a giggle.

Now that was interesting. Or was he setting up his defense for being crazy? The man knew exactly what he was doing, stealing from innocent young women and their families.

"I laughed at him and he didn't appreciate that I thought it was funny."

Suddenly, she looked at him strange. "Daniel, I have a favor to ask."

"What's that," he said, filling the coffee pot from his cantina, not really looking at her.

"Kiss me," she said.

He almost dropped the coffee pot as he raised his eyes to stare into her dark brown ones across the way in the early dawn.

"What brought that on?"

"You've always said that you would be honest with me and tell me the truth. I need to know something. After you kiss me, we'll talk about it."

Damn, she wanted him to kiss him and his chest seized with trepidation. Not because he didn't want to kiss her, but because he was afraid once he started, he would be unable to stop. There was only so much a man could resist.

He sat the coffee pot on the fire and then strolled over to

her. Was she delusional? Was this the result of being hit on the head?

Gazing at her full mouth in the flickering fire light, he wanted to kiss her. To show her that he'd been afraid. Even now he worried about her. To express his growing feelings for her in his kiss.

Sinking down on her bedroll, he pulled her gently in his arms, afraid of hurting her and yet knowing he longed for this kiss.

"You're certain about this?" he whispered, his mouth next to hers, his hand gently cradling her injured head.

"Yes," she said, her voice deep and throaty, her tongue swiping across her lips as she opened her mouth.

His mouth touched hers gently at first. Kissing the lower lip and then sucking it into his mouth. A sigh escaped her and she opened her mouth more for him. Not wanting to rush this kiss, he lingered at her lips before he delved into her mouth, his tongue dancing with hers.

As her breathing increased, she opened more for him and he took control of the kiss. Her hand reached up and wrapped around his neck to hold onto him as the kiss deepened and it was all he could to remain in control.

When had he started falling for the dangerous Miss Nellie? When had the spitfire worked her way into his heart?

He didn't want to let her go. The kiss had been perfect and he didn't want it to end.

Suddenly she broke the kiss and her eyes opened to stare into his. Breathing heavily, she gazed at him, her amber eyes wide. "You promised me you would always be honest with me."

"Yes, I did," he said, wondering what this had to do with kissing.

"Even if it hurts my feelings?"

"Yes," he said, growing more and more curious by the minute. But he knew he had to wait for her to ask her question.

"Am I horrible kisser?"

It was all he could do to keep from laughing, because he knew from her expression, this was a serious question and one she needed answered.

"No, you're not a horrible kisser. In fact, I enjoy your kisses a little too much. They excite me," he said, staring into her eyes, admitting his weakness for her. Did she understand how much she could excite a man?

"Oh," she said.

"Now you have to answer my question. Why are you asking?"

For a moment, she closed her eyes and released her breath. "Because the prince said I was a horrible kisser and that the people of Fort Worth hated me."

Unfortunately, he was right about the people in Fort Worth, but now Daniel was closer than ever to finding out what happened to Nellie. What made her into the woman she was today.

"Honey, stop listening to the man. Yes, he may have spent your trust fund, but he also could be just telling you that to make you feel horrible. And for God's sake, the man knows nothing about real love and marriage, so don't get me started on that. He's made a mockery of the institution."

The man was cruel and he'd made a lot of money on treating women badly, including her.

She gazed at him in awe, and for a moment, Daniel felt uneasy. Was she upset with him?

"Why are you such a good man?"

That was a simple answer. One he'd known for quite a while.

"Because I want my family, my children, and my wife to always look up to me and think of me as someone who showed them truth and love. It's important to me, for them to think I'm a good man. And it pleases me that you think so as well."

Maybe a little too much. Just gazing at her, his heart thumped wildly in his chest and his dick was like a rock. He was not what she wanted, but he was beginning to wonder if she was what he desired.

And the answer to that question would be a definite yes.

CHAPTER 18

*N*ellie's head pounded all day and she noticed that Daniel kept watching her. It was like he worried about her and her chest warmed at the thought.

All morning, she'd felt nauseous and even a little dizzy. The prince had tried to get rid of her and that just made her more determined than ever to catch him.

The memory of Daniel's kiss had lingered with her all day and when she glanced at his back, swaying in the saddle, she wondered what his hands touching her flesh would feel like.

And yet even now, she would start to quiver and the memory of that time would try to intrude. How could she have a normal marriage if her husband couldn't touch her?

It was late afternoon when they rode into Austin. The bustling town filled with people hurrying about their destinations. Everywhere she looked to see if the prince had arrived. But so far, she had not seen him.

They went to the telegraph office first, and her heart thawed at how Daniel was thinking about her interests.

"I thought you should do this now while we have the chance," he said, glancing back at her.

With her stomach rolling, she stepped off her horse and hurried inside. It took her about five minutes to send the telegram.

"What hotel are you staying in?" the man asked. "You might get a response this evening."

Daniel told him the name of a hotel and she gazed at him. The urge to stay in the same room with him filled her. Before, she hadn't wanted to be together, but now she wanted him by her side. And that shocked her.

She wanted to roll over and hear his soft breathing. To feel his body next to hers and she even wanted him to touch her.

After they left the telegraph office, they checked in at the hotel. Daniel only got one room and she didn't argue with him.

On the way to the room, he glanced at her. "I want to watch you and make certain you're all right. I can't do that with you in another room."

And that suited her just fine. In fact, it made her happy. He was worried about her and a heat spread through her like tiny tendrils of fire.

The exchange with the prince had frightened her and she liked the way Daniel had watched over her and cared for her all day. She couldn't remember the last time someone cared enough to check on her.

"It's all right," she said, knowing that tonight she was going to ask him to help her. Help her clear her demons.

They walked into the room and he set their saddle bags down.

"You feeling all right?"

"I'm all right. My head still hurts, but it's getting better."

He reached out and checked the bump on her head. "You've still got quite a goose egg there."

The warm feel of his hands on her head didn't bother her, and in fact, it felt good.

"Maybe we should find a doctor," he told her.

"Absolutely not."

She didn't want or need some man telling her she needed to go home to Fort Worth. What could a doctor do? It would just take time to heal.

"Why don't you stay here and rest. I'll have them bring you up a bath. I'll get us some dinner."

She smiled. That was exactly what she wanted him to do. She needed some time alone and a bath sounded heavenly.

"All right. But if you find the prince, I still get some time with him," she said. Though she had pretty much said what she wanted to him last night.

Tonight, she wanted time with Daniel. Time to see if she could get past her emotional wounds. Would he help her get over this fear?

He reached out and brushed her hair away from her face. "Rest, but don't sleep. I'm still worried about you not waking up."

A thrill spread through her at his touch. Maybe she was past her wounds. Over the revulsion that seemed to fill her whenever a man touched her.

Slowly he walked from her to the door. "I'll be back soon."

"All right," she called.

Twenty minutes later, they brought her bath up and she quickly shed her clothes and crawled in.

Lying back against the tub, she ran her hands over her

breasts and tried to think about how it would feel with Daniel touching them. The old memory crept back into her mind and for a moment she let it play out. Until she came to the most humiliating part and then she jerked and caused it to stop.

Three years had passed and still when the memory resurfaced, she was filled with hate and rage. And that's when she took it out on the people around her.

The water was beginning to cool when she got out and towel dried off. She pulled her nightgown out of her saddle bags and pulled it over her head.

Daniel walked in the door. For a moment, he stood staring at her with her gown on, her hair wet and hanging down her back. His sapphire eyes darkened as he gazed at her. Desire reflected from their gaze. And a heat began to spread through Nellie.

While his obvious desire left her nervous, it wasn't from the fear that filled her at the most inopportune times.

Quickly, she grabbed his shirt and slipped it on.

"I hope you don't mind me borrowing another shirt," she said, her voice husky.

"No," he said and set a sack of food on the table. "I think I'll hop in the bathtub real quick while it's still warm."

"Good idea," she said, watching him strip down to his long johns.

He stepped behind the screen and she heard him washing and even saw him throw his wet long johns up on the screen. In the last week, they had shared so much of their lives together and it felt natural. Like this was normal.

It felt like this was where she belonged.

And yet, it was anything but what she was accustomed to.

If someone had said she would be sleeping on the ground outside, trying to catch the man she was once engaged to, she would have ridiculed them.

If anyone would have said she was contemplating having sex with a Pinkerton man she would called them crazy, but he'd made her realize things about herself that no one else had ever noticed.

He understood her. And no one had even come close to understanding her before she met him.

When Daniel walked out from behind the screen, he had nothing but a towel wrapped around him. "I forgot my clean clothes."

With a nod, she walked to him, knowing he could reject her and she would be devastated, but he could also accept her advances. Which would he choose?

She stood in front of him and with trembling fingers she unhooked his towel and let it slide to the floor.

"What are you doing?" he gasped. "Nellie, it's hard enough seeing you in your nightgown. A man can only take so much."

With trembling hands, she laid them on his naked chest. "You understand me better than anyone. You have recognized that something bothers me. I'm hoping your touch will heal me. Make me a whole woman again. Cure me, Daniel."

A groan escaped his lips and he stared down at her. "Are you certain you know what you're asking me to do?"

"Yes," she whispered. "A man's touch brings up bad memories and causes me to tense. Help me, Daniel. Erase those images from my mind. Replace them with good ones."

Reaching out, he ran his fingers across her lips and she gazed at him.

"Tell me when you start to get anxious," he told her, standing there naked.

Then he slipped his shirt off her shoulders, and she stood in just her nightgown before him. Reaching down, he began to raise her long white nightgown over her head. When he finished, she was standing bare in front of him.

"Oh, Nellie, you have a body that will drive men to act irresponsible. Including me. I'm not the kind of man you want for a husband and yet here you are asking me to make you whole again. I fear the worst for me," he said as his fingers traveled from her neck down her shoulder where he lingered, down her arm to her hand, where he teased her palm. On her side, his digits skimmed her ribs, her waist and he leaned down to continue their path over her hip, her thighs, all the way to her feet.

"Your skin is like silk, your body curvaceous and rounded in all the right places."

He moved to her other leg and this time his fingers were traveling up. But he never touched her in intimate places, and so far, she had not had a reaction to him. All she could think about was how he was worshiping her body, showing her the beauty of what happened before two people joined together.

"Are you all right?" he asked as his fingers skimmed up her arm.

"Yes," she whispered, her hands lightly touching him, holding on.

His fingers skimmed over her chest, but he didn't touch her breasts. He moved his fingers rotating them around her breasts but not touching them.

"How does this feel?"

"Good," she gasped because it did. It was like he was

teasing her, by not touching her and she longed for him too. The urge to push them toward him was almost overwhelming.

"Touch me," she cried.

His fingers lightly touched her breasts, caressing them and then his fingers felt her nipples. When he touched her nipples, she felt the first warning signs.

"No," she cried. "Stop. Don't."

Immediately, his hands dropped from her and he stared into her eyes. "It's me, Nellie. Not anyone else, just me, Daniel. Focus on me."

His lips found hers and he kissed her gently and she felt her body relax. The images of the past seemed to fade away under his kiss and she sighed against him.

Slowly, he released her lips and stared into her eyes. "I'm going to start again. Every time it happens, we'll start over. We're going to keep trying until your mind recognizes that it's me. No one else, but me and you and that you want me to touch you."

And she did. With a nod, she pulled him to the bed. Maybe it would be better if they were lying down.

She lay on the mattress and he crawled up beside her. "Better?"

"Yes," she whispered. "Touch me, Daniel. Heal me. Make me whole."

A smile crossed his face and he began again. "I like it when you say my name."

"Daniel," she said just as she felt the demons from the past start to fill her mind "Daniel, I want you to touch me."

"If it becomes too much, tell me," he reminded her.

"I will, Daniel," she said, reinforcing his name on her brain. Trying to clear all the old memories of how she'd been hurt.

His fingers were on her breasts and then she felt his mouth there. She gasped as his mouth sucked her nipple between his lips.

And then the memories came roaring back like a tornado set to destroy her.

She tensed and he immediately released her. But this time she easily pushed them away. Closing her eyes, she tried to ban them from her brain.

"Are you all right?"

"Yes, it's getting better," she said. "Do that again."

A smile crossed his face. "With pleasure. It gives me so much enjoyment to suck your nipples, your breast."

Heat spread through her at the feel of his lips sucking on her nipples. Her fists clenched the bed sheets and this time when the memories started to flood her, she banished them. This was now. This was Daniel and this was not painful or humiliating.

This was pleasure. She wanted this with Daniel and no one else.

A moan escaped her and he moved his mouth to her other breast where he sucked the nipple into his mouth and then nipped it with his teeth.

The sensation sent spirals of desire scurrying up her spine and she closed her eyes and groaned. "Oh, Daniel."

His hand slipped between her legs and she gasped when he stroked her there. No one had ever touched her womanly folds.

There were no bad memories, only pleasurable ones Daniel was creating.

"I'm going to make you come, Nellie," he whispered against her flesh. "I want to see desire in your eyes and I want to hear you scream my name."

Why would she scream his name?

His fingers found the little button between her legs and he tweaked it sending desire rippling through her. Pleasure intensified and he continued to stroke her as a feeling built inside her.

An intensity that she didn't understand and a desire for more.

"What are you doing to me," she cried.

He plunged his finger inside her and she could feel an explosion building.

"Go with it, honey," he told her. "Let it happen."

And suddenly her body tensed and she was crying out his name. "Daniel."

"That's it," he said as he pulled her to him and held her while she experienced her first orgasm.

For a moment, she felt like she was falling to earth as she lay there in his arms, knowing she'd never experienced anything like that before. Emotion filled her at the realization this man was putting her first. Making certain her bad memories were beaten into submission and she had good ones that made her happy.

Daniel had healed her.

"Just wait, there's more," he promised her as he kissed the top of her head.

CHAPTER 19

*H*is mouth came down onto hers. As his lips moved over her mouth, delicious shivers roiled through him. The kiss Daniel bestowed on her had her clinging to him, his lips consuming hers, his tongue sweeping the inside her mouth as fire raced through him and he wanted more.

He wanted it all with this woman and that frightened him.

When she was completely limp, he broke the kiss though he didn't want to stop. A growing fire blazed between them as he stared into her earth-brown gaze. The feeling of swirling out of control consumed him and he had to take a deep breath to control his desire.

If he lost control, it would make her recovery even longer. And tonight was about healing Nellie from something in her past. Tonight was about showing her the beauty of what they were about to do.

"Any time you want me to stop, let me know. I want you to want me as much as I can hardly wait to get inside you. If you're not begging me to take you, then I'm not doing something right. And, honey, I want it to be right for you. I want tonight to wash away all your bad memories."

A whimper escaped her as Daniel placed his mouth on her nipples, sucking them into his mouth and nipping at the hard pebbles. While his fingers continue to stroke the nub between her legs, he wanted her to be controlled by the passion he was creating in her. The passion he hoped would make her realize that sex between two people was a beautiful event to be cherished.

Suddenly it was like the world exploded around her and she clinched Daniel's fingers as he slid them inside her and she screamed her pleasure, the sound echoing in the room.

"That's it, honey," Daniel said. "Come for me. Tonight is all about erasing your bad memories and replacing them with good ones. Show me that you're a beautiful woman who loves passion."

When Daniel thought she was languishing in the after-glow, only then did he place his penis between her legs.

Daniel stared into her eyes, knowing he needed her to tell him before they went any further if she was still a virgin. Had whoever harmed her raped her, as well? If so, he wasn't certain she was ready to have sex with him. But he would do whatever she wanted. Tonight was all about making her happy.

"I'm going to ask you a question and the reason I want to know is because of your past. Not a moral reason, but rather I want to know if you want to continue."

With Nellie, he was walking a fine line between healing her and causing her more pain and he wanted to do what was right for her.

With a sigh, she gazed at him, her eyes still dark with passion, her body soft and pliable. "What?"

"Are you a virgin?"

"Yes," she said and he knew she was being honest. Whatever happened did not end with them violating her. Thank God for that.

Now it was his job to make tonight great for her. A night to remember as the night she learned to love again.

"Are you ready for me to take your maidenhead? If so, it's going to hurt just a little, but once it's gone, it will never hurt again."

Why did this sound scary even to him? And yet, he wasn't certain he could stop if she said no. Did she realize she was giving him a precious gift? That she was letting him be the man who introduced her to making love. And that word scared him.

"Do it," she gasped. "Make me a woman."

That was all he needed to hear.

"Darling, I want tonight to be a good experience for you. No more bad ones. From here on out, I want you to remember this evening with pleasure and happiness."

And it was true. Every woman's first time should be memorable. Nellie had suffered a trauma and he wanted to erase the memories, fill her with good ones and destroy the men who harmed her.

Raising just a little, Daniel kissed her on the lips, nibbling at her bottom lip, trying to keep her distracted as he began to push his penis into her sweet womanhood. At first, she tensed and he feared her saying stop, but then she took a deep breath and relaxed.

"That's my girl," he said. "Relax. Let me show you the pleasure."

Slowly, he could feel her body stretching to accommodate him. When he felt the membrane, he reached between her legs and pinched her clit while he surged forward and the membrane gave from the pressure. A gasp escaped her.

"Are you all right?" he asked, hating that he felt the need to ask, but he would never continue if this was too much.

"Oh, yes," she sighed as she clenched his cock inside her.

Like a dance, they began to move and he could not believe the pleasure as she matched his movements, squeezing him and he knew he could not hold out for long.

Staring down at her, he wondered if she realized the importance of what they were doing? Did she realize that in the process of giving their bodies, he was resisting, holding back his heart and yet he couldn't help but know he was falling for this woman?

And she reminded him so much Louella. But in a better way. A vulnerable way.

Pleasure had her moaning, her breathing rapid and fast. They were each seconds away from coming and all he could think about was how much he hoped he had not hurt her in any way.

His hands were on her breasts and he tugged and pinched her nipples causing her to gasp as heat flooded his body. With a moan, she closed her eyes and let her head roll back.

"Hold on," he said. "I'm almost there."

How great would it be if this time they came together?

"Come with me," Daniel said.

She screamed as her body convulsed. Panting, Daniel never imagined that she would so loudly proclaim her pleasure. And he loved it. The woman was passionate and loving and…not the same woman who left Fort Worth.

Maybe the Nellie that everyone saw was the one that had been hurt so badly. That even now was dealing with the remnants of something bad that happened to her. His Nellie was a sweet woman, not the hateful bitch who made everyone uncomfortable.

With a last surge, his body exploded, and all he knew was that if he wasn't careful, this Nellie would claim his heart. This Nellie he would protect with his dying breath.

Daniel slipped off her and pulled her into his arms. Together they lay there, slowly coming down, their breathing returning to normal.

How could they return to being enemies? No, he didn't want to be her enemy. He wanted to be her lover and more. And that terrified him.

CHAPTER 20

Later that evening, they sat over the dinner that Daniel had gotten them and fed each other. The time slipped away with them laughing and talking and just being together. It felt so natural to be here with Daniel. The conversation was easy, the company pleasurable, and she liked this man so very much.

Nellie had never felt so wanted, loved, and cherished and yet neither one of them had said the words. It wasn't that she needed to hear them, but after the way Daniel had helped her, she felt certain he must feel something for her.

And she knew her feelings for him were growing by the minute.

The man had taken her introduction to sex slow and made certain she enjoyed the experience. If he was that caring when they had sex, what would he be like as a husband? Would he be as gentle and protective and caring?

No, he wasn't rich, but maybe that no longer mattered. Maybe for the first time in her life, she'd found a man who liked her for her brains.

After they finished dinner, they were lying in bed naked, staring into each other's eyes. Talking and whispering and just resting. He still fussed over her and her injury, but she no longer felt the effects.

"Tell me what happened," Daniel said. "What made you hate people so much?"

A trickle of fear and anxiety scurried up her spine. She had never told anyone and her biggest fear was that no one would believe her. The woman had told her it would be best if she kept this information to herself. And she had, because even the woman did not believe her.

Though sometimes she now wondered if that was to protect her son.

When Mrs. James walked in on the event, she acted like Nellie wanted what the boys were doing to her and she didn't.

Fear of no one believing her left her with the wound festering and brewing with hate that seemed to spew from her. Even Nellie recognized that many of her actions were to keep people away from her. That it stemmed from the hurt she'd experienced that day. How her trust in people had been completely broken after that experience.

"What?" she asked, knowing what he meant but needing time. She swallowed hard. Would he believe her? And if he didn't, how would she react?

Their time together had been so pleasant, and she didn't want to ruin it with talk of the event that jaded her. She didn't want to see pity in his eyes. She wanted this nightmare to go away and never touch her again.

"I promise to always be truthful to you. Now it's your turn to be truthful to me. What happened to you to make you so distrustful and pushing people away."

With a sigh, she closed her eyes and then opened them, staring into his sky-blue irises. She loved the color and wanted to just drift in them. But he deserved a response from her.

"When I was seventeen, a boy I really liked lied to me. We were not courting, but I trusted him. He told me that my girl-friends were waiting for me and he led me to a deserted building not far from the school."

A shiver rippled through her as she was transported back to that horrible day. "A lot of the boys hung out there and I naively believed that my friends had gone there with them. Only I was wrong."

A lump formed in her throat and she had to swallow hard to make it go away.

"It was after school, most children had gone home. When I walked inside there were seven boys standing there staring at me. Some of whom I considered to be my friends."

All the terror washed back over her. That was what hurt the most. The way her friends betrayed her.

"They tied my hands behind my back and then they began to remove my clothes." Tears welled in her eyes. No one had ever seen her cry and yet there was no stopping the tears this night.

"I struggled. I fought them. I kicked them, but they didn't care. I swore to them that I would tell their mothers and they laughed. A.J. told me that his father would tell him well done, son."

She took a deep breath and slowly released it. "I've never been so scared in my life. After they removed my top, one by one, they came by and touched my breasts. They pinched me and said that I may be the prettiest girl in school, but I had terrible breasts. They weren't large enough."

For months afterward, she had worried her breasts were not big enough. But now she didn't care. They were hers.

"It became a game for them to see who could out do the other and I was the object of their play," she said, her voice cracking, remembering all the hands on her body.

In some ways she was lucky, but the terror of that afternoon still remained with her.

"They were in the process of removing my pantaloons…" she said, tears streaming down her face as her mind replayed the horrible memories. The way she had screamed and cried and begged them to stop.

"What stopped them?"

"Mrs. James, Anthony's mother, came looking for him and when she found him, she was furious. She made them untie me and let me down. They had strung me up from a rafter. Then she glared at every boy there and told them to get home or she would tell all their mothers. After they left, she called me a trashy girl for allowing them to do this to me."

That was what hurt the most. That the woman had not believed her when she told her they had tricked her into coming into the building. That she wanted no part of this, but she pretended not to hear her side.

"Anthony did not defend me. He smirked at me and she told him not to ever marry a woman like me. That women like me would betray him and sleep with other men. She never once considered that her precious son had been one of the perpetrators who took advantage of me. It's always the pretty girl's fault."

How many other times had she been blamed for causing a

man's discretion when she had done nothing? One reason why she'd become such a bitch, it kept people, especially men from getting close. And lately, she kept everyone at bay.

"I did nothing to them. I never encouraged them or even gave them a second glance. And yet, Anthony's mother was certain it was all my fault."

"Why didn't you tell someone?"

The memory of dressing in that empty building, all alone, hearing the sounds of rats scurrying around her caused a shiver to race down her spine. The fear that they would return before she could leave.

"I cried all the way home. And when I got there, mother was in the living room hosting a group of ladies for tea. Papa was still working at the bank and my brother was off with his friends. When I went upstairs to my room, I feared if I told them, they would believe Anthony's mother and not me. They would think I asked for this and I didn't. So I kept quiet, which was probably the worst thing I could have done."

Daniel reached out and wiped the tears from her cheeks. "What happened when you returned to school?"

For a moment, she closed her eyes, remembering how the boys had treated her. How the girls had turned from her. How alone and betrayed she'd felt.

"The boys spread rumors about me. Said I was an easy girl who would let you touch her. And there were so many boys that tried."

Daniel's eyes widened and his eyes sparkled with anger. "What did you do?"

"I hired a man to teach me how to fight," she said. "Because with the rumors going around, someone, sooner or later, was going to try to get me. He taught me some simple ways that I could use that would keep them away. One day, I had to put those moves to use and if I had not been trained, I would have been raped."

"Tell me his name," Daniel said with a growl.

"Anthony," she said. "After all that he had done, he tried to rape me. But this time, I was prepared and I broke his arm."

The memory of them fighting flashed in her mind and how she had twisted his arm up and back until the bone snapped. Part of her felt bad, but after everything he had done to her, she felt like he deserved what happened to him.

Daniel started laughing.

"And yes, he screamed like I'd killed him," she said. "But after word got around to leave me alone. And the boys did. But as I've gotten older, I've gotten even with them for what they'd done. Papa doesn't ask why, but if I find out they're trying to buy a business or a house or get any kind of loan at the bank, I warn him against it."

"What does he tell them the reason they're declined?"

"He says Nellie said you aren't a good risk. I listen to my daughter."

A giggle escaped from her as she remembered seeing A.J.'s expression. "They can't ask why because if they did, I would tell Papa and they would be embarrassed and he would be furious."

Daniel pulled her into his arms. "I'm sorry that happened to you. Most of all, I'm sorry that you've kept this a secret all these years. Someday you need to tell your story. Let the people of Fort Worth judge these men's characters. Maybe it would help another girl in school."

Shaking her head, she thought of the humiliation she would suffer. The pain of what they'd done to her out there for everyone to see. How could she let people know what she suffered that day?

"Most of all, I think it would help you put this behind you. You're a beautiful, sensuous woman who deserves to be treated with respect. Those boys didn't treat you with respect and I doubt they would ever treat a woman the way she deserves."

Nellie reached up and grabbed his face. She pulled him close to her lips and rested her forehead against his. "Why are you so good to me?"

"Because you deserve to be treated well," he said. "This man believes in protecting women. If that had been my son, he would be sitting in jail."

All she could think was that she wanted him to protect her. To keep her safe and to cherish her the way he had his fiancée. She wanted that same care. She wanted Daniel.

CHAPTER 21

*T*he next morning there was a knock on the hotel room door and they glanced at each other as they sat drinking coffee at the little table, their eyes widening. Who could be at the door?

"The telegraph," Nellie said, jumping up and running.

Still in her nightgown, she stopped and gazed at Daniel. "Would you please answer the door for me?"

Before, she would have demanded that he deal with the people outside. But now she was asking and in a nice way. He was seeing a new, different side of the woman he adored.

This morning she seemed different. Lighter, her mood cheerful.

"Of course," he said, rising from the table where they were having breakfast.

It was a courier sent over from the telegraph office. He paid the man and then handed her the folded paper.

With a deep breath, she yanked it open and started jumping up and down. "He's alive. Papa is alive."

A smile spread across her face and she threw her arms around Daniel and hugged him. This Nellie he could so very easily fall in love with, but the other one frightened him and he feared she would soon return and show her mean manners.

"My brother is very funny."

She began to read the telegram from him. "Papa is all right. Come home, now."

"He's worried about you," Daniel said.

After last night, Daniel was beginning to be afraid. Afraid that he was falling for this woman and that she was so much like his last fiancé. And yet this morning, there was no sign of the sarcastic, mean woman who left Fort Worth. This morning, he wondered if he was getting a glimpse at the old Nellie, before the incident that changed her.

"That's sweet, but I'm going to help you get the prince. I want his crown."

"Let's pack up and get on the road. We are probably behind and we're about three days out of San Antonio. We've got to catch him there or he'll get away again."

They couldn't follow him across the country, and he would never take Nellie into Mexico. If they didn't catch him in San Antonio, he would insist on her returning home.

He watched as Nellie looked around at the hotel room.

"What are you doing?"

"I'm memorizing this room and all that we shared here. Last night was a special night and I want to make certain I never forget. I want to keep the memories I made with you."

A trickle of fear scurried down his spine. How could he separate the emotions of having the best sex of his life from the woman? How could he keep his heart intact when all he wanted was to take her in his arms and kiss her and let her know she mattered to him?

"We need to get going," he said. "I'm anxious to get to San Antonio."

She grinned. "Let's go."

"I think you should get dressed first," he said, smiling at her.

A giggle escaped her and she smiled.

Why was it they had so much fun together? They were relaxed and it felt like he'd come home. Not what he expected with Nellie. Quite the opposite.

Laughter filled the room as she grabbed her clothes from the saddle bags and pulled on the blouse, the riding skirt, and her boots. "I can't wait to get home and wear different clothes."

Louella had been a fanatic about clothes. Her father spent so much money dressing her in style. Would Nellie expect the same?

"What would you do if you had no money?"

She took a deep breath and released it. "I'd like to think I would learn to adjust. That if I was happy, that's all that mattered, but I don't know. I've never lived without money."

Oh, that's not how Louella would have answered that question. But it was truthful and that made him feel good. At least she was honest enough to say she didn't know how she would respond.

Maybe after their time together, she would look back with fondness and say he was the first man who taught her how to deal with her feelings and emotions. That with him, she'd learned the value of being a good person. That with him, she had learned to open up and give her heart.

That with him, she had put an ugly event in her life behind her.

A knock sounded on the door and they both glanced at each other.

Now she was fully dressed, their bags packed, and they were getting ready to walk out the door.

"Who is it?" he called.

"Sheriff," a voice said. He motioned her to move behind him. What reason would the sheriff have for visiting them.

Daniel pulled back the door gently and peered around.

"Is Miss Robinson with you?"

"Yes," Daniel said.

"She's under arrest for shooting and harming Prince Randolph Schmidt," he said, walking into the room followed by his deputy.

It was almost laughable, but Daniel knew better than to laugh in their face.

"What?" Nellie said, stepping from behind the door. "If I'd shot him, he would be dead."

That didn't really help her case, but Daniel knew she was frustrated.

Somehow the man had gotten to the law. Now it would take hours to get this straightened out, which would put him on the road far ahead of them.

Daniel tried to calm his rapidly beating heart when all he wanted to do was scream at them for being stupid.

"You know you've been had, Sheriff," Daniel said quietly.

The man's brows raised. "No, I don't. He said you would say something like that. He filed charges yesterday, but I haven't had time to come find you until this morning."

What if they had come in last night? Thank God, they didn't.

Daniel shook his head. "And I'm sure the prince has since left town."

"Said he was on his way to El Paso," the sheriff said. "But he's going to return in time for Miss Robinson's trial."

How long did the prince think they would keep Nellie? The man might not be very smart, but he was brilliant at throwing them off his trail. "Did he tell you I was a Pinkerton agent?"

"No," the man said. "Only filed the charges against Miss Robinson. Told us she was crazy."

Oh, when Daniel managed to finally get his hands on this man, he was afraid he wouldn't stop hitting him.

Nellie was beginning to get wound up as the deputy pulled her arms behind her back. The fear in her eyes and he remembered the last time her wrists were tied together had been when the boys from school abused her. He could see the terror building because they pulled her wrists together.

"Nellie, honey, they're lawmen," he said, trying to calm her.

"Did he tell you that he stole my trust fund and stood me up at the altar?" Nellie said as a deputy slapped the restraints around her wrists.

"No, he didn't mention anything about that, just filed charges against you."

"Daniel, they're trying to take me to jail," she cried, and he could see the panic building on her face.

He had to calm her down or they would see the beast inside her come out. "Honey, take a deep breath. I'm going with the sheriff and we'll talk about how this is affecting my investigation. How he's letting a criminal run loose. Give me some time and I'll have you out."

"But, Daniel," she cried. "I've never been to jail."

"Nellie, once they find out who your father is, I'm sure you won't be there long."

He walked over and touched her arm and squeezed her hand. "Remain calm. I'll be there soon. I'm not going to let anything bad happen to you."

And he'd kill anyone who hurt her, including those in the cell.

Tears welled in her eyes and then he watched as she seemed to gather herself within. God, he feared for the people in that jail. Bad girl Nellie would soon be unleashed on them. And she could be dangerous.

The deputy took her out of the room and he turned to the sheriff. "Now where were we? Have you checked the name of Fred Matthews? That's who your prince is and he's a real dandy. Nellie is one of several woman he's stole their dowry or trust fund and left them standing at the altar. He's not a prince, he's a jackass. And you, Sheriff, just fell for his line of lies."

The sheriff seemed to tense and Daniel realized maybe he'd gone a little further than he intended but he hated when lawmen did not check someone out. "I'm a Pinkerton agent and Nellie's father runs the Fort Worth National Bank. Not a man you want to anger."

"Come with me down to the telegraph office. I'd like to verify that you're really a Pinkerton agent."

Daniel knew the man was wasting their time, letting the prince get ahead of them. But what could he do?

"Of course," he said. "We were just about to catch the con

man and instead now we'll spend our time proving who we are. But you're the local law."

Three hours later, they finally released Nellie, who had the sheriff's jail in an uproar. Instead of sitting there quietly, she had the entire jail singing just to irritate the lawmen inside. When she walked out, the ladies inside cheered her on.

"Go get that prince, Nellie. Hang him," a woman called.

When she saw him, she smiled. "I knew you'd come for me."

"Of course," he said, holding her horse, wanting to get on the road. They had lost half a day and he planned on pushing them hard.

The sheriff stood outside watching them and Daniel knew he must have been paid, because no matter what Daniel did, he held them as long as possible.

"Hey, Sheriff, when are you up for reelection?" she called out.

"November, why?"

"Because I'm going to make a big donation to your opponent," she said, climbing up on her horse. "This town needs new blood."

Daniel chuckled and knew he needed to get her out of here before she said something that would land her back in jail.

"Let's go," he said. "We have a prince to catch."

CHAPTER 22

*L*ying by the fire that night, she watched the moon rise and worried about her and Daniel. Tonight, he seemed withdrawn and she wondered if he would make love to her. Oh, how, she wanted to be in his arms again, but he made it very clear they were going to rest and get up early tomorrow morning.

He was anxious to reach San Antonio before the prince decided to leave again. And she was distressed about her feelings for Daniel. When she gazed at him, it was like her body was attuned to his and heat spread through her.

Last night had been more than she ever expected. Last night had shown her the meaning of love and she wanted to continue those feelings with Daniel.

Though he'd been attentive and caring, she knew something troubled him and she feared it was her. Something about her and Louella was the same and she didn't understand what and she needed to know. There was so little about him that she knew. Only that he'd been engaged once.

"Tell me about your fiancée Louella," she said in the darkness.

"What's there to know? Things didn't work out," he said.

"Well, you must have loved her to ask her to marry you. What changed?"

Even in the darkness, she could see him tense and knew he didn't want to talk about his former fiancée. When a man like Daniel made a commitment, it was a promise, it was sacred, and it would take a lot for him to break it off. It was the kind of engagement she longed for.

Something bad had to have happened for him to end it. For a moment, she didn't think he was going to tell her, but finally he spoke.

"My sisters kept trying to warn me about her. They said she was cruel but I never saw her that way. Until the day I went into Richmond and witnessed firsthand how mean she could be. She stood on the street berating a small boy for accidentally sloshing water on her. She hit the child about the head and I knew this kid lived on the streets. He had nothing."

Nellie could not imagine that kind of life for a child.

In the darkness, the fire popped sending up a shower of sparks that cascaded down.

"Did you speak to her about her actions? What did you do?"

"I walked over and she was stunned to see me. The boy was a kid I spoke to every time I went into town. I asked him how he was doing and he seemed to perk up a little, but then she started telling me how this stupid child had spilled water all over her new dress. The kid was so embarrassed. But Louella had no sympathy for him. None whatsoever."

"It was an accident," Nellie said.

"Exactly," he said. "I asked the boy when was the last time he'd eaten and he told me two days ago. I gave him a twenty-dollar bill and told him that when he was sixteen to find me. I'd have a job for him."

Twenty dollars was a lot of money. "How did Louella react?"

A chuckle came from his side of the fire. "She turned her nose up and walked away, calling me a fool. Later, she told me that when we married, I would not be giving street urchins money. I didn't like her tone and asked her why she said that? She replied because they were disease riddled idiots that would soon die."

Nellie jerked when he said the words. "Wow. That's mean."

"Yes," he said with a laugh. "It was then I decided it was time to end the engagement."

"How did she react when you told her?"

Daniel started to laugh. "She confirmed my worst fears by throwing the biggest tantrum. I went to her house, and she threw herself in the floor screaming. It was like watching a child. Afterward, her father kicked me out and told me to never come back."

That would have made her Daniel angry. And yet he didn't mention how it affected him personally. Surely, he must have been sad or distraught after she acted the way she did.

"Didn't that break your heart?"

There was a moment of silence and she heard him draw a quick intake of breath.

"At the time, my father was trying to tell me how to live my life. My sisters were telling me that Louella wasn't right for me. When her father kicked me out, I was so angry and knew I needed to get away. It felt like everything was falling apart. Then I saw an ad that the Pinkertons were hiring and I applied and got the job. I left Richmond behind and haven't been back in three years."

As she lay there, she realized they both had their own demons. And yet this man was the kindest person she had ever met. He'd shown her how she was acting out because of her own personal hurts. He'd helped her deal with her pain and made her into a whole woman again. A woman who could love.

And she loved Daniel.

He had never hurt her. He'd been honest and kind, and as much as she wanted to marry a rich man, her heart was telling her no, he was the one who would make her happy. He's the one who would always protect and honor her. He's the one who would never try to destroy or humiliate her.

But could he love her back?

"Do you still love Louella?"

He gave a little laugh. "Oh no, I realize that ending that engagement and leaving Richmond was a good plan. But I do miss my family and my father is getting older. After this, I may go home for a while. See my crazy sisters, hug my mother, and try to make amends with my father."

But there was no mention of her. As much as she had fallen in love with him, it didn't seem he felt the same way. He wasn't including her in his future life and that stung.

With a sigh, she rolled away from him and a tear slid down her cheek. Why couldn't a good man love her?

As much as she tried to change, it didn't seem to matter.

With a sigh, she wiped her tears away. As soon as she could retrieve her trust fund, she was going home. And if the people of Fort Worth still treated her like they had before, she would leave.

Maybe she needed a new beginning.

"Nellie?" he said in the darkness.

"Yes," she replied.

"Thanks for asking how I felt about Louella. I'd not thought about my family in a long time. It's time I went home to see them. You made me realize how much I miss them."

"Good, you're welcome," she said. How she would have loved to have that many sisters. But she was fortunate to have her brother.

But that didn't help him realize that she was in love with him. And he didn't love her. All she wanted was for Daniel to return her love. After everything that had happened to her, she'd finally figured out what she wanted—Daniel.

CHAPTER 23

*E*arly the next day, they rode through the streets of San Antonio. It was just after noon and Daniel was ready for this adventure to come to an end. It was so hard to be around Nellie and not drag her into his arms and kiss her senseless.

Oh, how he wanted Nellie, but she wanted a rich husband, a man who was beyond wealthy. And he wanted a wife who married him because she loved him, not because of his money. His family was well off and yet that was one of the problems with Louella. She wouldn't have looked at him twice if she'd thought his family didn't have enough money to make her life comfortable.

But that wasn't love and he wanted a woman who would love him. Someone who made him a better man and had his best interests at heart.

Nellie reminded him so much of Louella and he feared giving his heart to another woman like her. Though even now, his heart had feelings for Nellie that he refused to acknowledge. He couldn't fall in love with her, she would only cause him more pain.

And she would never agree to living in Virginia.

They pulled their horses to a halt in front of the hotel, and she threw her leg over and dropped to the ground. They each pulled their saddle bags off the animals and carried them inside.

Together they walked through the door and up to the counter of the hotel. It was a nice two story with a diner off to the side and a livery in the back. He had stayed here once before and knew it was a safe place.

"May I help you folks?" the attendant asked.

"We need two rooms," he said.

Behind him, he felt her tense, but she didn't say a word. Would she throw a fit like Louella or would she accept they were not sleeping together? For his own sanity, they couldn't be together again or she would own his heart and soul.

"Here," she said, pulling out her reticule. "This will pay for my room."

She handed the man the necessary bills.

"I was going to pay for it," he said, glancing back at her.

"No, I need to pay my own way."

There was a coldness about her response and he could see she was hurt. But if they stayed together, he would have to admit he loved her and he couldn't. She was not for him.

"Could you please have a bath sent to my room," she told the man behind the counter.

"Of course," he said.

"Where do we take the horses?" she asked.

The woman was truly wanting to be on her own and she was cutting him out of her life. If he didn't want to sleep with her, then she could handle the breakup. But he didn't want to end it with Nellie. This wasn't what he wanted. He wanted to give her everything, but he feared he wasn't enough for her.

"There is a stable in the back."

"I'll take care of the horses," he told her and he could feel her stiffen.

Didn't she understand if they continued sleeping together, he could get her pregnant? Then he would feel obligated to marry her. As much as he wanted her, she didn't want him.

"I'll carry my saddle bags up to my room," she said.

"Wait and I'll carry them up for you," he said and he could see the sadness in her gaze. He'd caused that pain.

She shook her head and he could see the tears pooling in her eyes. "It's all right. I can do it."

With that, she turned and walked up the stairs, carrying her saddle bags.

While he could see that she was upset, it was for the best. And yet already he was missing her. Already he was regretting his actions. He didn't want to hurt her; he only wanted what was best for them. He wanted what was best for her.

After he took care of the horses, he decided he should see if he could find the prince. Walking the streets of San Antonio, he looked where he thought he might have gone to meet people. The man was excellent at finding his victims.

Not far from the Alamo, he found a restaurant and had a bite to eat. It was the first time he'd eaten alone since he started traveling with Nellie. And he didn't enjoy being by himself.

He missed her.

Couldn't she see he was trying to do what was best for

them? Yet, his heart missed her being by his side. The closeness, the way she smelled and yes, the sex they experienced.

If he thought about the two of them entwined together, he would soon find his way back in her arms. Was he crazy?

Maybe he should talk to her. Tell her his reasons that they should no longer share a room. Because if he had sex with her one more time, he would be ensnared to her forever.

He ordered some pralines and paid for his meal. On the way back to the hotel, he listened to a band playing Spanish music and he watched the couples dancing. As he strolled down Main Street, he felt lonelier than he ever had.

What had he done?

Nellie should be here beside him, but he let his fear guide him. He had to put space between them or he would never let her go.

As soon as they caught the prince, and they would catch him, he had made the decision to return to Virginia. It had been too many years since he'd been home. It was time.

And yet, the thought of leaving San Antonio without Nellie was gut wrenching. But he was certain she would find a man that would give her everything she wanted, and it wouldn't be him.

This trip had shown him a different side of Nellie, one he really liked and knew he could fall in love with. But she would never agree to be a Pinkerton agent's wife. No, she wanted the husband with the big bank account and that wasn't him.

After they had their con man, they were taking the train back to Fort Worth. This way there would be no sleeping on the trail. No being together. No risk of Fred the Prince escaping. But first he had to find the man.

Slowly he walked to the hotel and climbed the steps to his

room. He wanted to give her the praline he'd bought her, but there were no lights on in her room.

Hopefully, she was sound asleep and not out wandering the streets looking for the prince.

He stopped in front of her door and listened but heard nothing. No, he didn't want to wake her and have her answer the door in her nightgown. That would be break his resistance faster than her coming to his room. No, he had to be strong and walk away.

With a sigh, he turned and headed down the hallway.

Women were a pain in the ass and yet this one had gone from being a pain to being a someone he could fall in love with, who had attached herself to his heart. And every day they were together, it would be harder and harder to leave her.

All he could do was think about Nellie, and yet, he knew it would be better for them to be apart.

When they returned to Fort Worth, she would find herself a wealthy husband. But tomorrow they had a prince to catch.

CHAPTER 24

*W*hile sitting in the bath, Nellie concocted a plan. A plan on how to catch the prince. After she dressed, she opened the door, and glanced out. She didn't see Daniel. She hurried down the stairs and went to the desk.

"Where can I buy a newspaper?"

The man handed her one from behind the counter and she paid him.

"Where is the nearest dress shop," she said. "A secondhand store preferably." Her funds had dwindled, but she had enough to carry out her plan if she was frugal.

"Two blocks over," he said.

"Thank you," she said as she hurried out the door. Sitting on a bench, she looked through the society pages of the newspaper. With a chuckle, she found the information she needed.

An hour later, she purchased a nice dress and hurried down to the newspaper office, hoping to get there before they closed.

"Can I speak to Miss Brickner?" she asked in the tiny entry

way of the building. In the back, she could hear their printing presses preparing tomorrow's paper.

"May I tell her who is calling?"

"Nellie Robinson from Fort Worth," she said. Hopefully the society columnist would recognize her name.

A few minutes later she was ushered back.

"Miss Robinson," the woman said cheerfully. "Nice to meet you. What can I do for you?"

How much should she tell her? How much would be leaked out before the next victim?

"I'm here in San Antonio on a mission. Prince Schmidt is in town and I'm covering his arrival for the newspaper. I was wondering if you could get me into tonight's gala at the Rodriquez home."

The woman smiled. "Of course." She pulled out a pad and wrote down the address of the home where the gala was being held. Then she penned a personal note.

"I'm sure Señorita Rodriquez would be honored to have you. It is formal."

"Of course, and I brought a dress with me," she lied. She would have to run back by the dress shop and purchase one.

"I'm so excited to meet the prince tonight," the woman said. "I hear he's dashingly handsome."

"Oh, yes," she said, thinking he was also a thief.

She glanced at the address and knew she would need to hire a driver to take her. The thought of inviting Daniel entered her mind, but she couldn't be with him right now. She needed time away to steel her heart against him.

"So I'll see you there, tonight," Nellie said.

"Oh, yes, and I look forward to introducing you to everyone."

"That would be wonderful," Nellie said, standing, trying not to act over excited, but thrilled at how her plan was coming together.

The evening dress she asked the lady at the dress shop to hold was still there when she returned. Quickly, she picked out shoes to go with it and hurried out the door. She had a ball to prepare for.

Two hours later, she stepped out of the carriage in front of the elegant home. Built in the Hacienda style, she loved the rounded arches and the tile roof. The home appeared inviting and she hurried up the steps to the front door.

When she arrived, the butler looked at her note and allowed her in.

"Thank you," she told him. "I'm from Fort Worth and I'm covering the event for the newspaper."

The man just gazed at her, but didn't say a word as she walked in.

The ballroom was down a beautiful staircase that ended on the edge of the dance floor. Already, couples were swirling around the floor, the swish of satin and silk could be heard as the couples twirled.

"Hello," a voice said. "I'm Angelina Rodriquez. Miss Brickner said she had invited you."

Nellie took her hand in hers. "Thank you so much for letting me attend. I'm here from the Fort Worth paper to cover your beautiful gala. Also, I'm covering the prince."

The woman smiled. "Of course. He is dancing with all the women. I can't believe I have a prince in my home."

The woman would be sadly disappointed when she learned the truth.

They stood off to the side of the dance floor watching the couples swirl around to the waltz.

"What paper do you write for?"

"The Fort Worth Telegram," she said. "We're doing a big article on the prince and so I'm following him."

The music suddenly changed from a waltz to a fast-paced Mexican dance. Everyone cleared the floor except for the dancers who performed the Jarabe Tapatío, a courtship dance.

While they were watching the costumed dancers flirt with one another, the woman leaned over. "I like to mix in my culture with the other dances."

"It's beautiful," Nellie said, wishing she could see where the prince had gone. If he saw her, he would walk out the door.

"Excuse me, I'm going to find the prince," she said as she walked away.

The man was dangerous and she wanted to make certain he didn't get away. She also did not like the idea of him finding and choosing another victim.

As she gazed around the room full of people, all watching the dancers, she glanced up and the prince's eyes were narrowed on her.

A smile crossed her face and she gave a little wave. His heart must be thumping out of his chest right now. And he would be searching the room for Daniel, but he wouldn't be here.

Maybe she should have told him where she was going and invited him along, but now was not the time to be thinking of Daniel.

They walked toward one another in the large circle of people.

"What are you doing here," he hissed.

"Got out of jail and here I am."

He grinned at her and she knew her instincts were correct. He had paid the sheriff to hold them up.

"It's been so long, I don't think I know you," he said.

She laughed. "I've been trying to find you. Heard you were looking for another victim," she said with a grin. "All these women need to know about Prince Schmidt."

His face was turning red and she realized he was furious she was here.

"Now, Prince, why are you getting all angry. Don't want another girl to be left at the altar like you did me. Or heaven forbid, her trust fund be stolen. All you have to do is give me my money back and we're good."

"Not going to happen," he said between gritted teeth. "Leave or you're a dead woman."

"Oh, Prince, how ungrateful you are," she said. "You really need to work on your attitude."

A growl erupted from him just as the music ended.

Knowing she had to do something now, or regret attending tonight, she picked up a fork lying on a table and hit against her glass. "May I have your attention."

People turned and gazed at her in wonder before everyone finally quieted.

"This is Prince Randolph Schmidt otherwise known as Fred Matthews, not from Habsburg, Netherlands, but Baton Rouge, Louisiana. He just likes to pretend he's a prince as he steals young women's trust funds and leaves them at the altar at church. Now you've been warned about his treachery, I'd like to ask the law to step forward and arrest him. There is a Pinkerton agent in town searching for him."

She waited and no one seemed to be approaching him. Dear God, where were all the lawmen in town?

"Where's the law?"

"Someone went to fetch the sheriff," a man yelled out. "He's on his way."

Just then the prince turned, his face contorted in rage, his fists clasped. "You have done so much to harm me. But not anymore."

He reached out and grabbed her and pulled a gun out of his pocket at the same time. Pointing the gun at the patrons around them, he snarled. "Get out of my way, now."

Knowing her life depended on it, she turned and kicked him, but his grip was too much. She doubled up her fists and hit him over and over, but it didn't faze him. She tried all the tricks she'd learned in her fight class, but they did nothing.

"If you don't stop, I'm going to shoot you right here in front of everyone. Do you understand?"

"I'm not leaving with you," she said.

"The hell you aren't," he said as he lifted her and threw her over his shoulder.

Then he swung the gun at everyone in his path.

"Get the hell out of my way," he said, "or I'll shoot you."

With disregard for her modesty, she flailed her arms at his back. She kicked and screamed.

"Get Daniel McClintock at the Union Station Hotel. Tell him what's happened. Tell him the prince has Nellie."

"Shut up," he said as he slammed the back of her head against the wall and once again the darkness descended over her.

CHAPTER 25

A pounding on the door awakened Daniel from a sound sleep. Something was wrong.

Jumping up, he wondered if it was Nellie. Would she come to his room to convince him to have sex with her? The idea sent a chill through him. There was no way he could turn her down.

Opening the door slowly, he was surprised to see the sheriff and a deputy stood there waiting for him.

"Daniel McClintock?"

"Yes," he said, his eyes widening, his senses coming to full alert.

"Do you know a Nellie Robinson?" the sheriff asked.

"Yes," he said, fear seizing him. Was she dead? Had the prince killed her?

His heart pounded and he feared the worst. What had the woman gotten herself into this time?

"She went to the Rodriquez gala and there she had an encounter with Prince Randolph Schmidt. He's taken her and she screamed your name and said to notify you. What do you know about why he would take her?"

"Son of a bitch," he said. "She's supposed to be asleep across the hall."

What the hell? He goes to bed and she goes out to a party without him? Hunting down the prince, obviously. Only she'd found him which was better than Daniel had been able to do.

"When did this happen?" he asked, wondering how long he had before the man killed Nellie.

"About thirty minutes ago."

The thought caused his chest to squeeze with pain, his fists tightened. He had to find her before the man ended her life. God, he'd fallen in love with her and now she was in danger.

"Let me put some pants on and we'll go," he said, closing the door and rushing back into the room.

Quickly, he dressed, shoving his six-shooters into his holster.

Damn, she'd left the hotel tonight. While he'd been out eating and searching the streets, she'd gone to a ball where the prince was once again holding court. The woman was smart and he should have realized what the prince would be doing tonight.

Finding another victim.

When he walked out of the room, the men were waiting for him.

"Any idea where he might have taken her?"

"None," the sheriff said.

"All I know is that she told the crowd about him and he pulled a gun on her and carried her out of the ballroom."

How the hell did she get into the ball? Why was he even asking himself that question? The woman was smart and she could finagle an invitation to the best parties. But she didn't have a dress, did she?

They hurried down the stairs and it took Daniel a few minutes to get his horse from the livery and saddle it.

Riding down the deserted street, he went first to see if the man's entourage had arrived yet.

"Did a circus arrive in the last few days?"

"Not a circus, but a group of men with a big tent and trailer," the deputy told him. "We were wondering what it was for."

"That's the fake prince's entourage. Let's go there," he said.

There was no way the prince would take Nellie to his sordid followers. He would take her somewhere out of town where he could kill her.

The deputy led him to the edge of town where tents were set up with the official seal of a Habsburg prince. The man knew how to run an elaborate fraud.

The entourage had set up camp close to the river. Daniel pounded on the trailer door and the man who told him the prince was going to San Antonio answered.

"What are you doing here?" he asked sleepily.

"Where is she? Where would the prince have taken Nellie?"

The man leaned out the entrance and glanced around the grounds as if he wanted to make certain everything was all right.

With a sigh, he shook his head. "Sometimes he goes out to the edge of town along the river and practices shooting."

"What direction?"

"The south side where the Mission San Francisco de la Espada is located."

Daniel had a good idea where to find the old mission. "If you're sending me on a wild goose chase and she is killed, you're a dead man."

The boy licked his lips. "I'm not. But I suggest you hurry."

The three men climbed onto their horses and hurried out of the yard toward the mission.

In the darkness, it was hard to drive the horses faster than they could see. The closer they came to the mission, the more he pulled back on the reins. He didn't want to gallop into where they were holding Nellie and be shot.

That wouldn't do her any good.

As they rode onto the grounds of the mission, he noticed a light in the distance. A flickering flame that indicated a campfire.

"No," a female voice screamed. "I'm not going to help you. You know the Pinkerton agent will hunt you down if you kill me." That was Nellie's voice.

"That Pinkerton agent is the very reason I'm holding you. Once both of you are here, you'll be out of my hair forever."

"They're here," Daniel said quietly.

He pulled his horse to a stop and glanced at the two men who were with him. "From here, we walk."

They slid off their horses and dropped to the ground. In the darkness, they all checked their handguns to make certain they had plenty of ammunition.

A rage had been burning inside Daniel since they left the entourage. Anger at the prince for taking Nellie and even more at her for leaving without telling him where she was going.

And now he could see her in the light of the fire, tied to a tree. How was he supposed to rescue her without the prince shooting her?

"Let's see if we can sneak up behind him," Daniel said.

"No, he has guards surrounding them," the sheriff said.

"We can't get to her without getting rid of them first," the deputy said.

"I'll take the farthest two and you get the others," Daniel said. "Then we'll see how this plays out. Whatever you do, don't let him harm Nellie."

That was his biggest fear.

The three of them spread out in the darkness, each moving silently toward their targets.

If the prince killed Nellie, he would die a very painful, slow death. Daniel moved toward the men in the darkness, hoping to kill them before the prince was alerted they were here.

CHAPTER 26

*N*ellie knew she'd made a huge mistake going to the ball without Daniel. If he'd been by her side, then the prince could not have taken her. But even if she died tonight, she had warned the women of San Antonio about the fake and his scheme of stealing their wealth.

Hopefully they would spread the information across Texas and the prince would no longer harm other women.

At first, the prince treated her fine, but she could see him growing anxious. The fear in his eyes, the way he paced about camp, and she knew he realized he was in trouble. He realized the law would soon overrun him like a herd of cattle.

Ranting, he talked to himself. "How will the Pinkerton agent know where to find you if I don't send him a note? I need both of you here, so I can end this pursuit once and for all. At dawn, I'll tell him where you are, but by then you'll be dead."

Terror scurried down her spine. But then she thought of Daniel and hope filled her. If he received her message, he would come.

A smile spread across her face and she had no concerns that eventually Daniel would find her. If no one from the ball went to get him, then it could be even longer before he arrived. But eventually, he would come.

And he was sure to be angry with her.

After the way Daniel acted, what did he expect? She wasn't going to just sit in the room and wait for him to locate the prince. While soaking in the tub, the perfect way to find him had come to her and here she was.

Tied to a tree on the edge of San Antonio, near an old fort, hoping he arrived before the prince decided to end her life.

Maybe it wasn't the perfect plan, after all, but she had found the man they were hunting.

What if the prince killed Daniel? How was she going to react if he killed the man she loved?

She worried her bottom lip as she thought of Daniel getting shot by the prince.

"You know, if you hurt a Pinkerton agent, they will come down here and swarm this place looking for you. You'll not get away with killing him or me. You're wasting your time."

The man swirled around, and for a moment, she feared he was going to hit her.

"Shut up. Accidents do happen, and believe me, I'm going to make this look like you shot him. You're such a bitch, it will be the perfect ending to your mean life."

What had she done to cause such hate in a man?

Tears welled in her eyes. People would believe she killed Daniel. No one would ever think the Prince of Habsburg was capable of murdering two people. After all, he was part of the monarchy. They would believe the lie.

With her boot, she began to draw a message in the dirt, not

certain that it would still be here when they found her body, but she had to try. She could not let him get away with this awful treachery.

"What did I do to make you hate me so? I thought you wanted to marry me. That I would be your queen?"

The man started laughing. "Women are so gullible when you tell them you're a prince. Their eyes get big and they see dollar signs and they think they're going to be part of the royal family. What I do to them, they deserve, and I have no regrets."

The man was crazy and yet what he said was true. She had been awestruck by the fact he was royalty and she would be a queen. Everything had been a lie and she'd been a fool not to see it before now.

"You're right. I was blinded by the thoughts of being a queen and marrying a prince. But another man showed me the folly of my beliefs and now I see you for the scum you are. You're prancing around with a crown on your head when you have nothing but hate in your heart. You're a sad little man."

His face turned red in the light from the campfire.

"Shut up," he called again, "or I'll shoot you right now and that damn Pinkerton agent can find your body slumped against the tree."

"That would spoil your plan," she said, deliberately antagonizing him. "After all, I'm supposed to be the bad guy here. Oh, by the way, my father and my brother would never believe I killed a Pinkerton man. They will hunt you down."

Suddenly he turned, pulled out his gun and fired a shot, hitting the ground close to her feet.

"The next time, I won't miss," he said.

With a sigh, she smiled. If Daniel was around, now he

would know where to find her. Glancing into the darkness, she tried to see past the light into the shadow of the trees. There were the remains of an old mission out there and she knew the prince's men surrounded them.

Looking up at the stars, she sighed. If she were going to die here tonight, she prayed Daniel would not be harmed.

Maybe even now, Daniel was on his way to rescue her. Maybe even now, he was somewhere beyond the firelight.

The tree was scratchy against her arms. Could she wear down the ropes that bound her? While the prince paced the area, she rubbed the ropes binding her wrist against the bark.

Suddenly she felt fingers on the rope and realized that someone was behind her, helping her.

"Don't move," Daniel whispered. "The sheriff is also here."

A smile spread across her face as her heart leaped in her chest. He had come for her. Daniel was here.

"When I tell you to get down, do it."

Suddenly, the sheriff stepped into the firelight. "Drop your weapon, Prince."

"Not on your life," he said as he pulled out his gun and aimed at the sheriff. The man dropped and rolled as Daniel stepped out from behind the tree, his pistol cocked.

"You have a choice. Do you want to live or are you ready to die? Drop your weapon," he commanded.

The man pretended to put his weapon down but then he suddenly charged Daniel. The two men fell to the ground and the prince smashed his fist into Daniel's face. They rolled and Daniel was on top as he whipped the pistol grip against the prince's head.

The man bucked, sending Daniel flying and leaped to his feet. He ran toward Nellie and she screamed and ran in the opposite direction into the darkness. She could hear him not far behind her and knew Daniel would be giving chase.

"Stop or I'm going to shoot," he screamed at her, but she wasn't listening. "Stop."

And then she saw a broken tree limb in front of her.

"Don't shoot, I'm stopping," she cried as she stepped over it. She moved off to the side and waited. Just as he reached the tree limb, she raised it just enough that he went sprawling onto the ground, his gun discharging.

She felt the bullet whiz by, scrapping her arm. A stinging pain radiated down her arm. That was close.

Daniel stepped over him and kicked the prince's gun out of his hand. The hammer of his gun made a loud noise in the dark. "Don't move; you're under arrest."

The sheriff came running up and he rolled the prince onto his stomach and snapped the handcuffs around his wrists.

"Are you all right, miss?"

"I think so," she said.

"You're bleeding," the sheriff said and she saw Daniel's face whip around to her.

"You've been shot," he said as he cursed. "Sit down."

"I'm all right," she said and suddenly the world seemed to grow woozy. "I'm all right."

Her knees gave way and she collapsed onto the ground. "Really, I'm all right."

Daniel huffed. "Let me help you back to the light and we can see how bad it is."

She could feel her blood dripping down her arm and she tried to see the wound in the darkness.

Daniel wrapped his arm around her waist and helped her back to the fire. The sheriff and the deputy were bringing the prince — Fred—with them and with every step, she felt a little more lightheaded.

"Are you mad at me?"

"Furious," he said.

"You left me in that room all alone. What was I supposed to do? Sit there and wait for you? It was while I was soaking in the tub that it came to me. The prince would be working any balls that were being held. So I went to the gossip columnist at the newspaper and she gave me an invitation to the gala tonight. And there was our prince, dancing away."

As her world spun crazily, she glanced at Daniel. "Besides, you left without me. I couldn't have asked you if I wanted to."

The man was silent for a moment. "Do you know what it's like to have the sheriff and his deputy pound on your door at eleven o'clock at night and wake you from a deep sleep? They told me you were screaming my name as he carried you out of the gala. I've never been more frightened."

A smile crossed her face. She was about to pass out.

"If I hadn't, you would never have found me," she said.

When they stepped into the light, she glanced down at her arm. The realization then that another inch and she could have lost her arm hit her. The bullet had torn through her muscle, leaving a hole where it went in and out.

Nausea rolled through her at the sight.

"Have I ever told you that I don't do well at the sight of blood?"

"No," he said, staring at her.

"I think I need a doctor," she said as her knees gave way and she slumped to the ground. The blackness descending over her as she heard his cry.

"Nellie!"

CHAPTER 27

The next day the sun was high in the sky as Daniel paced the doctor's waiting area. Last night he'd almost lost Nellie. No, the wound was not life threatening, but the prince could have so easily have killed her. He had watched from the shadows and saw the prince shoot the ground beside her to threaten her. He saw her determination to make certain that Daniel knew she was there.

All in all, Nellie had been extremely brave and the town of San Antonio would be brimming with the news of the capture of the prince. Hopefully, her being a hero would get her good attention and she'd find a husband quickly.

Someone she wanted, not him.

The newspaper reporter, Miss Brickner, had already been by and he'd told her the story. She promised to share the article with the Fort Worth paper.

Last night had scared him badly. This was the woman he loved, and she'd been so close to death. And yet, he couldn't say those words to her.

And he couldn't be around her much longer.

He sent a telegram to Fort Worth to let her brother know she needed help getting home. His train had already left. By the time he arrived, Daniel would be gone.

Already he had contacted the Pinkerton headquarters there in San Antonio. Captain James Smith had come over and the two of them had a long talk.

Daniel would be leaving on the next train heading east to Atlanta and then on to Virginia. It was time for him to take a break and gather his thoughts. Right now, he wasn't certain of what he wanted. Only that he had to get away from Nellie or beg her to marry him.

And she needed to get home where he hoped the people of Fort Worth would open their hearts and their arms to the girl who had gone through so much. The girl who had captured the prince.

No longer would the man be stealing money from women and promising to marry them. His days would be spent in jail for a long, long time.

The doctor had been in surgery working on her arm, trying to put it back together. The wound had been more serious than they first believed and she was lucky not to lose her arm. She would stay here in his hospital until her brother arrived.

Licking his lips, Daniel felt nervous. How would she react when he told her he was leaving? Would she throw a tantrum like he expected?

The doctor's wife appeared at the door. "She's awake now and anxious to see you."

With his hat in his hand and his heart on his sleeve, he followed the woman into the back.

"She's doing very well. The arm is extremely sore, but she's going to be all right," she said.

He nodded, afraid to speak. There was so much he needed to tell Nellie and yet all he could think about was how much he loved her.

The nurse pulled the curtain back. "Look who is here to see you. You may sit in a chair next to the bed, but don't get near her arm."

"All right," he said as the woman walked away and pulled the curtain behind her.

"How are you?" he asked.

Groggily, she gazed at him and then reached out and ran her right hand down his cheek. "I'm alive, thanks to you."

His chest tightened at her touch. Oh, how he wanted to throw himself across her body and confess to her his feelings. How frightened he'd been that he almost lost her, but he couldn't. As a man of honor, he wanted her to have what she wanted and it wasn't him.

"Did I dream it? Is the prince behind bars? You came and saved me."

He took her hand in his and squeezed it. "No, you didn't dream it. He's facing charges here and in Fort Worth. They plan to extradite him to Fort Worth in two days."

He didn't tell her that she would be on that same train with her brother returning home. Not yet. Right now, he wanted to enjoy these last few moments with her before she learned of his leaving.

"It's over," she said with a sigh.

"Yes, and I found a large sum of money in his saddle bags. I think it is your trust fund. I have put it in a bank for you."

Her eyes widened. "The prince didn't spend it?"

"No," he said, smiling. "You are once again a wealthy woman."

A frown crossed her face. "I'm so glad you found my trust fund. But…"

Tears filled her eyes.

"There's no reason to cry. You captured the criminal, you saved your future, and had quite an adventure you can tell your children about some day."

He had to get out of here or he was going to ask her to marry him. As much as he loved her, it would be better if she married someone who could give her the life she wanted.

He stood and let her hand slip from his. A gut-wrenching pain seized his chest as he let her go.

"Your brother is on his way to San Antonio and should arrive tomorrow."

"Oh," she said, her brows drawing together in a frown. "I thought you and I were going to return to Fort Worth together."

Shaking his head, he knew he had to hold it together a little while longer. "My train leaves for Atlanta this afternoon. Then I'm going home to Richmond to see my family for a bit. I've taken a leave from the Pinkerton's. I don't know if I'll go back."

Her mouth fell open and he saw tears shine from her eyes and yet she quickly looked away.

If she started crying, he would be lost.

"I see," she said. "You've wanted to go home to your family."

"Yes," he replied, wishing she would throw the biggest tantrum, anything to help him remember she was like Louella. But, damn, she didn't. She took the news of his leaving calmly.

"Thank you, Daniel, for everything you've done for me. For helping me realize I can be a good person. For seeing the best in me, and most of all, for catching the prince and rescuing my trust fund."

She swallowed and he could see she was really trying not to cry. He wanted her to beg him to stay. He wanted her to say that she loved him, but she didn't.

"Whenever you come back to Fort Worth, be sure to stop by and say hello," she said.

He would never return to Fort Worth. Never. Too much heartache lived in that city.

"Of course," he said.

She reached out and grabbed his hand and squeezed it. "I hate that you're leaving, but I understand. I'll never forget you."

Tears clogged his throat. Where was the damn tantrum he so desperately needed her to pitch? Didn't she realize that by proving to him that she had changed, she was making it so much more difficult for him to leave?

Time to go. Now. Or never walk away from her again.

"Good-bye, Nellie," he said, his voice rough.

"Bye, Daniel," she whispered barely saying the words.

With one long last stare, he turned and walked out of the area, pushing the curtains around the bed away.

Damn, double damn. What in the hell was he doing? He was doing what was best for both of them. He was doing what was best for Nellie.

CHAPTER 28

A week later, Nellie stepped off the train in Fort Worth. The last week had been both joyous and devastating. Joyous because she'd gotten her trust fund back and helped capture the prince. Devastating because of Daniel's departure.

How could he leave her? Did he not feel the love she felt for him? Even now, her heart ached because he'd left her.

When she first saw her brother, she burst into tears, frightening him.

"Are you all right?" he said, rushing over to her bed in the hospital.

"I'll be fine. I'm just so happy to see you," she said, and he had leaned back in surprise.

They had talked for hours and then gotten on a train home. She watched as the new Pinkerton agent loaded the prince onto the train. Then the agent had walked over and smiled at her.

"Daniel said to give you this," he said and pulled the prince's crown out of his saddle bags.

Joy filled her and a smile crossed her face. A giggle escaped her and her brother stared at her like she was crazy.

"He said you would know what to do with it."

Oh, yes, she knew what to do with the fake crown.

"Would you like to ride with us to the jail?"

"Yes, I'd like that very much," she said, thinking it would be an appropriate way to end her journey. She only wished Daniel was here riding beside her. Oh, how she missed him. It was like a piece of her heart had been removed.

As people with luggage bustled around the train station, a man brought a horse around and she stepped up into the saddle. Her brother smiled at her. "Welcome home. You can do this."

A tear trickled down her cheek. Yes, she could ride with the prince down the jail, but what she really wanted was Daniel to love her like she loved him.

"Thanks," she said and placed the crown on her head.

"How's that for royalty."

Her brother laughed.

She had been surprised to learn that the Fort Worth Telegram had ran the same article as the San Antonio paper that told how she had revealed the prince for the thief he was.

As she followed Fred and the Pinkerton agent, she was shocked to see the people lined along Main Street and they waved and cheered her. Stunned, she realized they were applauding her. The people of Fort Worth who had treated her so badly were now cheering her and she couldn't help but give a little sniffle.

Happiness filled her and she wiped the tear that trickled down her cheek. It felt good to be welcomed home.

"Nellie," she heard someone call her name and saw Mrs.

Griffin walking along the side of the street. "Dear, would you please give me an exclusive interview. I'd love to speak to you."

The woman was a notorious gossip and Nellie wanted to stay away from that kind of sensationalizing, but maybe she should tell what happened to her. Maybe it was time for the people to understand why she had acted the way she did. Maybe her experience would keep it from happening to another young girl.

"Of course," she said. "How about tea tomorrow at the Griffin Hotel."

The woman smiled. "So happy you are alive and glad you're home."

"Thank you," Nellie said.

"Were you badly hurt?"

Nellie held up her arm that was in a sling. "I was shot, but I survived."

They rode all the way to the jail and then she watched as Fred turned and glared at her.

"Fred, enjoy jail," she called. "It's the kind of kingdom you deserve."

A sneer curled his lip and he spat on the ground before they jerked him up the rest of the stairs and he disappeared behind the door.

It was over.

Suddenly her mother and her father were at her side and she slid off her horse and fell into their arms.

"I'm so happy to see you," she said. They hugged her to them and she cried. "Take me home."

A little girl came running up to her. "Welcome home, Nellie."

It was such a sweet gesture and Nellie removed the fake crown from her head. "Thank you. Here, you can have this. I don't want to see it ever again."

The little girl's eyes grew wide and she gasped. "Thank you."

Then she turned and ran down the street to her friends. "Look what she gave me. I have a crown."

Turning to her parents, together, arm in arm, they walked down the street and then climbed in the carriage to go home. A servant tied her horse to the back.

"Are you all right," her mother asked.

"Yes and no," she said. "Oh, Mother I've fallen in love with a man and I don't think he loves or wants me."

She leaned her head on her mother's shoulder and cried her eyes out. How could Daniel not want her?

Later that evening, her sister-in-law Tessa and her brother came over for dinner. Tessa was going to have that baby just any day now and Nellie wondered how it would feel to be pregnant with Daniel's child.

The thought made her heart swell, but then she realized it would never happen. The man didn't want her.

Eventually, her father and mother retired for the night and she sat in the parlor with Tessa and Seth. Tessa had propped her feet up and Nellie knew she was tired. It was so cute the way her brother doted on his wife and she felt a little jealous. They were so in love, and she wanted what they had.

"Why didn't Daniel return home with you?" Seth asked.

Because he didn't love her the way she loved him was all she could think, but she knew there were other factors as well.

"He had not seen his family in three years and decided it

was time to visit. He needed a break from being a Pinkerton man after this case."

Tessa tilted her head and gazed at her. "Did you tell him you were in love with him?"

How did she know? Was it written on her face that she had fallen in love while she'd been gone?

Nellie took a deep breath and released it slowly. "No, neither one of us said we loved each other."

"But you do love him, don't you?"

"Yes," she admitted, her heart wrenching from the pain.

"Did you have sex with him?"

Her brother gasped and stared at his wife. "That's not something you ask someone."

Tessa shrugged. "Men are difficult and they're strange. It took you forever to admit that you loved me. She needs to hear that Daniel might be in love with her, but maybe he mistakenly thinks she wants someone else."

Something struck Nellie and she felt a tingle along her spine. "When you think of me, what do you think I want in a husband."

"A rich man," Tessa said automatically. "You were supposed to marry a wealthy prince."

Her brother gazed at her. "Is Daniel rich?"

"Of course not, he's a Pinkerton agent. I'm sure they make decent money, but not what I would consider rich."

Shaking her head, Tessa made a grunting noise. "If I were Daniel, I would think I'm not what you want. 'I'm not rich. I'm just an ordinary man.' Love means accepting that person for better or worse, richer or poorer. Would you marry Daniel knowing he wasn't rich?"

Nellie started to cry. Why did she seem to tear up all the

time? "Of course, I would. I love and miss him terribly. I can't stop thinking about him and my heart is breaking."

Her brother took her hand. "And you never told him you loved him?"

"No. It was like suddenly things between us became full of tension. And when he came to the hospital to tell me good-bye, I did my best to make it easy for him."

Why had she not been fierce with him and demanded he stay with her. Because she wanted her husband to love her for who she was and not for throwing a tantrum to keep him.

"Wow, that doesn't sound like the old Nellie," Tessa said. "This trip really changed you."

"Yes," she said softly, wondering if what Tessa said was true. Did Daniel love her and he'd just not said the words, thinking she wanted something else?

And Tessa was right, the old Nellie would have thrown a fit and called him all kinds of names. In some ways, it would have been easier to do that than to let him go.

With a sigh, her brother gazed at her. "You need to go after him. You should get on a train and go to Virginia and tell him how much you love him. If he loves you, he will know as soon as he sees you and he won't let you come back."

The thought was daunting. "But what if he doesn't want me?"

"Then you will know. Won't it be better than sitting here the rest of your life wondering if you let the man you love get away?" Tessa said.

Nellie thought for a moment. Did she want to sit here, letting the only man she ever cared for leave. Maybe he did think he wasn't rich enough for her, but that wouldn't be true.

Being with Daniel was all the riches she needed.

She glanced at her brother and sister-in-law and smiled. "I can't leave tomorrow because I have something I must do, but I think I'm leaving for Virginia day after tomorrow. I think I'm going to go tell the man I love how I feel."

They stood and the three of them hugged.

"Remember, even if it doesn't work out, you'll know for certain," her brother said.

"Ohhh…yes, we're here for you. But before you go, I think we better call the doctor. My water just broke."

Nellie screamed. "Yes, I get to see my niece or nephew before I leave."

Seth's face turned white. "Dear God, we're not at home. Wake Mother and Father. I think their first grandchild is being born here."

CHAPTER 29

*D*aniel had been home for two weeks. His sisters were creating all kinds of mischief around the house while he spent most of his days with his father. His mother kept kissing him and tearing up, so happy to see him.

And he had to admit, he was enjoying being around his family. Only one problem, he missed Nellie. He missed her obstinance, her determination, and in the end, her spirited softness.

His heart ached for her. His body craved her and his mind kept playing tricks on him, making him believe he heard her voice. The ring of her laughter, her giggle, and even her snappiness.

He would never forget that last day when he said good-bye. She had not reacted the way he expected and that made him doubt his decision. If she had thrown a fit, he would have known for certain she was just another Louella. But instead, she had calmly told him good-bye and wished him luck.

All the way out the door, he had doubted what he was doing. And even now, he wanted to get on that train and head back to Fort Worth. He wanted to go to her and ask her what she wanted. Did she want him?

And he also worried about her.

What if she wasn't healed from the bullet wound? What if she was treated badly by the people in Fort Worth? What if she needed him?

But then he would remind himself he wasn't who she wanted. She wanted a rich man, and while he had wealth, he wanted a woman who loved him for who he was. Not because of his bank account or his land holdings. He wanted someone who loved him.

Today, he was out in the fields helping his father and the workers cut cotton. It was harvest season and they needed to get it off the plants and to the mill before the winter rains came. Being busy kept his mind off what he was missing.

His father was too old to cut the cotton, but he directed everyone from the edge of the field, telling the men to sack it up and put the cotton in the wagon. When the wagon was full, it would head to the mill where they kept a tally of how many pounds they received from their plantation.

Maybe a wealthy plantation owner was not supposed to work the land, but in order to get the cotton picked in a timely manner, Daniel would do what he needed to. It didn't matter to him who was picking it, as long as the job was done.

Dust rose from the road and he thought his mother must be bringing them lunch. During harvest, she often brought them a meal. It was a welcome break.

He glanced again and realized it wasn't his mother. A man was driving a team of horses and a beautiful blonde woman was sitting in the back of the carriage.

His chest squeezed and his heart began to pound furiously.

"Nellie," he said, rising from picking cotton. "Nellie."

He began to run to intercept the wagon. "Nellie."

She glanced over and saw him in his filthy work clothes. Not exactly how he wanted to look the next time he saw her, but he didn't care.

Why was she here?

The carriage came to a halt and she stepped out just as he reached her. Without thinking, he pulled her into his arms and lifted her high. "I'm so happy to see you."

"Me too," she said in a soft whisper.

He set her on the ground and held her tight, not caring if he messed up her dress. "I've missed you so much."

"I've missed you," she said, her voice choking up. "I had to come. I have to know."

"What?" he said, wanting to kiss her so badly, not willing to let her go. If he could, he would never let her go ever again.

She leaned back and gazed at him. "Daniel McClintock, I love you. I have loved you since Waco. If you don't love me, then I'll have this nice man take me back to town and catch the next train home. But I have to know if you love me as well."

A smile spread across his face, and he covered her mouth with his and kissed her like he would never let her go ever again. Finally, he released her mouth and stared into her stunned face.

"Nellie, I have loved you since before Waco, but I thought you wanted a wealthy man, so I left. I didn't think I was good enough for you."

Shaking her head, she gazed at him. "You could be as poor as a church mouse, and as long as I'm by your side, I don't care. All I want to do is spend the rest of my life with you. We can live in a hovel, beg on the streets or both work to earn a living. Money doesn't matter as long as you love me."

Relief filled him and a grin spread across his face. Then he was releasing her and dropping down to one knee. "Nellie Robinson, will you marry me and make me the happiest man in Virginia. I love you with all my heart and if you hadn't shown up here today, I was heading back to Texas next week to find you. All I want to do is spend the rest of my days with you."

Crying, she pulled him up and to her. "Yes, I want to be your wife. I don't need a prince or money or anything but you by my side."

Daniel layered his mouth over hers and kissed her deeply. Relief flooded his body and happiness filled him. He released her and she reached up and caressed his face.

"Oh, Daniel, I've missed you."

A grin spread across his face. "You're my love."

At a noise, Daniel looked up and saw his father was standing beside his mother and his sisters and all the workers in the field. When had they arrived?

"Daniel, who is this?" his father asked, smiling.

"Nellie Robinson, my fiancée," he said proudly. "We're getting married."

His family surrounded him, and he could see the approval in their eyes. "Welcome to the family," his father said.

His sisters jumped up and down for joy. "Does this mean you're going to move to Virginia?"

Nellie glanced at Daniel. "Wherever Daniel is, that's where I'll be."

Joy flooded him as he realized his wife loved him for him and nothing else.

His mother wiped tears from her eyes. "Well, come on up to the house. We need to break out the sherry and celebrate. Finally, the day I've been praying for has arrived."

Large oak and pine trees had hidden the house from view. As they walked up, Nellie gasped at the mansion.

"Is this your home?"

Daniel grinned. "Yes, love, this is my home. Along with all the land you can see."

She turned and smiled at him. "It didn't matter. I would have loved you if you lived in a tent."

"I know," he said. "I love you, Nellie."

"Love you, Daniel. I'm so glad my sister-in-law Tessa told me to come."

"I'll have to thank her the next time I see her," he said. "How soon can we marry?"

"Could we have a small ceremony with just the family here at your home?"

"I would love that, Nellie. But I would marry you anywhere."

"Marry me, here, Daniel. Marry me where we will be spending our life together."

Unable to resist, he kissed his soon-to-be-wife. The prince had brought them together, but love would keep them united forever.

CHAPTER 30

*S*adie glanced around at the women sitting in her parlor and felt tears well in her eyes. So much had changed in the last two years. They were all married. Sadie's little one was crawling.

Tessa's baby, two months old, lay against her breast. A boy that her husband, Seth, proudly proclaimed would be the next champion sharpshooter.

Time would tell.

Rose was home from New York and her belly was rounded with her and Hayden's first child.

"When are you returning to New York?" Tessa asked quietly as her baby slept on her chest.

"Not until the baby is six months old," she said. "We want him to be around his nana and papa before I go back to the opera. So far, they are being very understanding. At least until someone younger with a better voice than mine comes along."

Shaking her head, Sadie glanced at her. "Who could sing better than you? They are lucky you are in their production."

Rose had fought so hard to fulfill her dream that she should enjoy it as much as possible.

"Maybe," Rose said, rubbing her hand over her stomach. "I stayed until the end of the season, and they were thankful for that. If we time it right, we could be there at the beginning of the next season. I love what I do, but Hayden and this little one are more important than singing opera."

Tessa patted her son on the back and then she gave a little shiver.

"Did you read the article Mrs. Griffin wrote about Nellie? Dear God, I had no idea she had been almost raped by the boys in school. And Mrs. Griffin didn't waist a moment in naming the boys," she said.

"It was so brave of her to come forward and tell everyone why she acted the way she did," Rose said, shivering. "I don't know if I would've had that kind of courage. And for them to get away with it for all these years."

"I heard the sheriff had spoken to each of them, including the mother who walked in and found them. She should have called the law right then," Sadie replied. "I can't imagine finding my son acting so horribly."

Rose turned and glanced at Sadie. "Would you call the law if your boy was doing something so heinous?"

"Yes, because he would need to know his actions were wrong and how he humiliated and hurt the girl. At least I hope I would have the courage. If you don't, then he thinks his behavior is all right and would continue."

The three women were silent for a moment each contemplating how they would handle that with the small babies they loved so much.

"Let's all hope we raise our boys to be good men who treat

women the right way. I'm with you, I will personally take a strap to my son if he acts in that way with a woman," Tessa said, gazing down at her baby boy, love reflecting in her gaze.

They sat, contemplating how in two years ago, their lives were so different.

"I brought a letter from Nellie that I want you to hear," Tessa said and she handed her reticule to Sadie. "You read it, Sadie. It's inside."

Sadie pulled out the letter.

"Dearest friends, I know in the past I hurt each one of you and I sincerely want to apologize. Though at the time, I was hurting so badly that I let my actions make others hurt as well. Again, I apologize and I hope you can find it in your hearts to forgive me.

I'm loving Virginia and my husband makes me want to be a good wife and mother every day. Yes, we're expecting our first child next summer and we're both ecstatic. Though I miss my family in Texas and my sweet nephew who arrived right before I left, I know my place is here in Richmond.

It's a new beginning for me and you'll be happy to know I'm making friends and not enemies.

May you all have wonderful lives with your husbands and children. If I ever return to Fort Worth, I want to see all of you and meet your children.

Nellie"

"Wow," Rose said. "That doesn't sound like the old Nellie."

"No," Tessa said. "The experience of chasing the man who stole her life and left her at the altar really changed her. Not to mention her husband. She's made me understand that sometimes when people act mean, there's pain causing them to act so ugly. She was a completely different person when she left for Virginia. I kind of miss her."

"I forgive her," Sadie said. "Because of her, I met the man I love, and look at my life now."

"I forgive her as well," Rose said. "Though I still wish she would not have told my father where I was hiding. But she didn't know what he would do. It's time to forgive her and put the past behind us."

"Yes," Sadie whispered.

"Oh, I had to forgive her because she's my sister-in-law, but now I understand her much better. And she loves our little boy."

Rose patted her stomach as she smiled at her friends. "Can you believe we're all mothers or soon-to-be mothers? Who would have known that being a bad girl could make our lives turn out so happily? I'm so blessed with a profession I love, a husband I love even more, and now this wee one."

"Well, personally, I hope you have a girl. Tessa and I have boys and we need some girls in our family. So it's up to you," Sadie said.

Tessa teared up. "We are truly blessed to have the love of each other, our husbands, and our children. I'd be a bad girl all over again if I knew this was how my life would become."

"Me too," Rose said.

"Aww, me as well," Sadie said.

The three women gazed around the room and smiled. They were blessed.

WHEN I STARTED THIS SERIES, I wasn't certain how long it would become. I knew the first three women, but I never considered writing Nellie's story. Not until my editor insisted.

And frankly, it became one of my favorites in this series. I hope you enjoyed Daniel and Nellie's story. In the spring of 2022, I might write his sister's stories, but I haven't decided yet. Let me know what you think. As always, thanks for reading my books.

PLEASE LEAVE A REVIEW

Did you enjoy the book? Reviews help authors. I would appreciate you posting a review. Click here to leave a review.

Follow Sylvia McDaniel on Facebook.

Sign up for my New Book Alert and receive a complimentary book.

The First Book In Bad Girls of the West

Sadie ever wanted was to be accepted. Being the second richest young woman in town, she would've thought that wouldn't be a problem. But money didn't buy the right connections in high society or the friendships she craved—acceptance by a group of ladies in town who considered themselves society's darlings.

And yet today, she received an invitation to a picnic with none other than Nellie Robinson, the mayor's daughter. The girl who seemed to control the local young women. The one person whose words were often cutting and cruel, who decided which girls were accepted, and which ones were not. The leader of the clique.

The woman was mean if ever she had met one. Could she be ready to accept Sadie?

Preparing for the outing, Sadie, wore one of her nicest dresses with a stylish hat covering her dark hair and even an umbrella to keep the sun off her ivory complexion.

As she waited outside the house in the summer sun, she wondered if the woman would stand her up. Send her an invitation and then never arrive. It had been known to happen before.

A man in a dark suit, driving a buggy, came around the corner. The poor man must've been sweating buckets in the hot Texas heat. Nellie Robinson leaned out the window and waved to her.

"Sadie, let's go," she said.

Hurrying to the buggy, she lifted her skirts and climbed in. "Nellie, it was so kind of you to invite me."

The girl smiled. "Well, I thought it would be the perfect day for a picnic out at the springs on the other side of town. Cook prepared us a lunch. Who knows? We might even dip our toes into the water to cool off."

Sadie couldn't believe how kind Nellie was being.

"Sounds lovely and tell your cook thank you for preparing the meal," she said.

With a wave of her hand, Nellie dismissed the very thought. "That's her *job*. Daddy pays her to cook for us."

Not wanting to upset her, Sadie didn't say a word at how privileged she sounded. Her own servants were more like family.

"Are you attending the ball this weekend?"

"Yes," Sadie said, excitement rushing through her. She had a new gown she couldn't wait to wear.

Nellie's blonde hair blew in the wind as she turned her brown eyes on Sadie. "You know, Levi Griffin, the most eligible bachelor, is said to be attending. His mother, the newspaper columnist, Betty Griffin, is trying to find him a woman to marry this year. Though the man keeps insisting he's never marrying."

Sadie had seen pictures of the man. Handsome, dark hair,

and emerald-green eyes, but if he didn't want to marry, why would anyone force herself on him?

"Why doesn't he want to marry?"

Nellie shrugged. "Who knows, but he is the best catch of the year, and I plan to snag him."

There wasn't a man Sadie could think of that she wanted to snag. Was she wrong wanting them to catch her? To court her? To vie for her affections?

As the buggy rolled through the area known as Hell's Half Acre, Sadie gazed around. Her father had never approved of this part of town. He'd said it was filled with criminals and cowboys drinking and gambling. Papa was always one for propriety and she was stunned that Nellie's driver took them this way.

"Look at that saloon girl," Nellie said. "Despicable. Earning her living on her back."

An uneasy feeling skittered down Sadie's spine. Why had she wanted to be with this snobby young woman? She didn't like Nellie and yet here they were on their way out of town to the springs. She changed the subject. "Did you purchase a new gown for the ball?" she asked her hostess.

The girl smiled. "It's exquisite. Mother had the dressmaker get the latest patterns from New York. It will be beautiful and I'll be the prettiest girl at the ball."

Sadie gave her a weak smile. "I'm sure you will be."

"Oh, look here is the springs. I love this place."

This pond, with a small waterfall from a river that fed the lake, had lush vegetation and big oak trees. A natural spring, the water was clear and cool.

The driver pulled the buggy to a halt, set the brake, and stepped down to help them alight. The place was deserted and an eerie feeling skirted up Sadie's spine. Almost a warning.

"Robert, place our picnic on the ground and then do not be within sight for a while."

He spread a blanket out and then set a basket down. "Yes, ma'am. Anything else?"

"Just wait on the road. I'll call you when I'm ready to go."

"Yes, ma'am," he said and crawled into the wagon and drove off, leaving them alone.

They both sat on the blanket, then Nellie opened the basket, and fixed a plate. She handed it to Sadie. "Bon appétit."

After Sadie had taken a few bites of the food, she smiled. "Delicious," she said. "I'm so glad we're doing this."

An impertinent smile crossed the young woman's face. Since their days in school, this was the friendliest Nellie had ever been to Sadie. Maybe the young woman had changed.

"You've been alone since your papa died?" Nellie asked.

"Yes, my servants have been with me for years, so they protect me."

"You can do whatever you want."

"Not really. My maid watches over me very carefully."

"That's not the same," Nellie said. "You're free."

What she meant by free, Sadie didn't have a clue, but she wasn't about to argue with the woman.

They finished the meal and then Nellie turned to her with a wicked smile. "Let's go swimming."

"What? Ladies don't swim," Sadie said.

Nellie stood and began to remove her clothes. "This lady does. Come, no one is here. No one will see us. We can cool off in the water."

The thought of cooling off sounded wonderful. It was a

hot summer day, and Sadie did want to belong to Nellie's group of friends.

"All right," she said as Nellie ran stark naked into the clear, sparkling spring water.

Glancing around, Sadie hung her clothes on a bush and then ran as fast as her long legs would carry her into the water. The cool wash was like a breath of fresh air. Nellie was swimming out to the center of the pool and Sadie reluctantly followed her. She was a weak swimmer at best.

When they reached the middle, Nellie grinned at her. "Isn't this refreshing?"

"Yes," Sadie admitted.

Nellie went even farther out and Sadie followed, wondering how far she intended to go.

When they were near the small waterfall, she laughed gleefully. "Race you to the bank."

She took off and Sadie knew she would never catch her. When she reached the bank, Nellie grinned at her.

"Not much of a swimmer, are you?"

"Not really," she said.

"Race you to the falls again," she said, taking off splashing her arms. By this time, Sadie was winded and arrived a lot later than Nellie.

They paddled about in the water and then Nellie glanced at her. "I never really thought you would come out here with me."

How did she respond without sounding desperate?

"I've wanted to be your friend for quite some time," Sadie told her. "You've never shown any interest in being sociable with me. And I thought this would be a good chance to get to know you."

The girl smiled. "My daddy is the richest man in town. I'm very careful about who I choose to be my friends."

Sadie nodded. She could see that.

"Even though your father left you a lot of money, you're kind of an oddball. An outcast, even though you're quite beautiful."

"Thank you," Sadie said, hoping she meant that as a compliment.

"But we'll never be friends. In fact, you're going to hate me," she said with a wicked grin.

A trickle of alarm spiraled through Sadie as she wondered at her statement. What did she mean, hate her?

"Last one back remains behind," she said and took off toward the shore.

Stunned, Sadie glanced at her. *Last one back...behind?*

Dear God, no!

Immediately, she swam as fast as she could. By the time she reached the shore, Nellie had grabbed *all* the clothes, the picnic items, and was making a naked dash to the buggy.

When she reached the waiting vehicle, she shouted to her driver. "Let's go." The man stared at her nude form as she screamed at him. "I said let's go."

"What about the other young woman?"

"We're leaving her behind."

The man shook his head and climbed into the buggy. At the shore, Sadie stood and watched as her nemesis drove off, taking with her every stitch of clothing she'd been tricked into doffing.

Dear God, what did she do now?

Grab Your Copy Here!

Also By Sylvia McDaniel
Western Historicals
A Hero's Heart

Second Chance Cowboy

Ethan

American Brides
**Katie: Bride of Virginia

Angel Creek Christmas Brides
**Charity

**Ginger

**Minne

**Cora

Bad Girls of the West
Scandalous Sadie

Ravenous Rose

Tempting Tessa

Nellie's Redemption

The Burnett Brides Series
The Rancher Takes A Bride

The Outlaw Takes A Bride

The Marshal Takes A Bride

The Christmas Bride

Boxed Set

Lipstick and Lead Series
Desperate

Deadly

Dangerous

Daring

**Determined

Deceived

Defiant

Devious

Lipstick and Lead Box Set Books 1-4

Lipstick and Lead Box Set Books 5-9

Lipstick and Lead Box Set Books 1-9

**Quinlan's Quest

Mail Order Bride Tales

**A Brother's Betrayal

**Pearl

**Ace's Bride

Scandalous Suffragettes of the West

**Abigail

Bella

Mistletoe Scandal

Southern Historical Romance

A Scarlet Bride

The Cuvier Women

Wronged

Betrayed

Beguiled

Boxed Set

The Debutante's of Durango
The Debutante's Scandal
The Debutante's Gamble
The Debutante's Revenge
The Debutante's Santa

** Denotes a sweet book.

**Want to learn about my new releases before anyone else?
Sign up for my New Book Alert and receive a
complimentary book.**

USA Today Best-selling author, Sylvia McDaniel obviously has too much time on her hands. With over seventy western historical and contemporary romance novels, she spends most days torturing her characters. Bad boys deserve punishment and even good girls get into trouble. Always looking for the next plot twist, she's known for her sweet, funny, family-oriented romances.

Married to her best friend for over twenty-five years, they recently moved to the state of Colorado where they like to hike, and enjoy the beauty of the forest behind their home with their spoiled dachshund Zeus and puppy Bailey. (He has his own column in her newsletter.)

Their grown son, still lives in Texas. An avid football watcher, she loves the Broncos and the Cowboys, especially when they're winning.

www.SylviaMcDaniel.com
Sylvia@SylviaMcDaniel.com
The End!